Cheri Weatherwax checks to make sure she has all the necessities for her hasty wedding:

Something old

☑ Does Jake's dad count? After all, the sweet old dear is the one who arranged this whole marriage deal for me.

Something new

☑ Well, I will have a brand new check for one million dollars in my purse.

Something borrowed

☑ The groom. I *do* have to give him back in a year.

Something blue

☑ Me. If I make the mistake of falling in love with Jake...

Dear Reader,

Oh no—dating! It's something I actually have to think about, just like a lot of women. And so far the men I've run into seem to have a lot more in common with Clyde Canasta than Mr. Right. "Who's Clyde Canasta?" you ask. He's a character from Renee Roszel's first Yours Truly novel, *Brides for Brazen Gulch*. Luckily—for you and for heroine Lorna Willow—he's *not* the hero of the book. That would be Clint McCord. Now *he's* a date I could deal with!

Of course, after dating comes (maybe) marriage. Unless you're Cheri Weatherwax, heroine of Lori Herter's *Blind-Date Bride*. In that case marriage—and a million bucks—comes first, but if dating your husband were really like this, I think more couples would meet at the altar and take it from there. Check out this latest in her MILLION-DOLLAR MARRIAGES miniseries to see what I mean.

And don't forget to come back next month for two more books about unexpectedly meeting, dating... and marrying Mr. Right.

Enjoy!

Leslie Wainger
Senior Editor and Editorial Coordinator

Please address questions and book requests to:
Silhouette Reader Service
U.S.: 3010 Walden Ave., P.O. Box 1325, Buffalo, NY 14269
Canadian: P.O. Box 609, Fort Erie, Ont. L2A 5X3

LORI HERTER

Blind-Date Bride

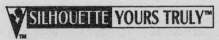

Published by Silhouette Books

America's Publisher of Contemporary Romance

To my husband, Jerry, the best date of all.

 SILHOUETTE BOOKS

ISBN 0-373-52025-5

BLIND-DATE BRIDE

Copyright © 1996 by Lori Herter

About the author

LORI HERTER

Have you ever been on a blind date? I have, years ago. (No, that's not how I met my husband, Jerry.) My two blind dates fizzled, as most do. Going on a blind date is taking the risk that you'll spend time with a stranger feeling bored, nervous, perplexed, or all three. *Marrying* a blind date is taking this risk to the extreme—which is why I thought it would make a great premise for a book.

Jasper Derring, the matchmaking millionaire father introduced in *How Much Is that Couple in the Window?* (2/96 YT), selects Cheri, a down-on-her-luck pizza parlor waitress, as the prospective blind-date bride for his son Jake in my third Yours Truly, *Blind-Date Bride*. Jasper's final touch is to send them off to an island together for a year. As you'll see, the couple grows perplexed, nervous, and highly frustrated—but never bored.

I really enjoy writing for Silhouette's Yours Truly line, because I can create likeable, everyday heroines who find themselves thrown into madcap situations with heroes they never dreamed they would fall in love with. My MILLION-DOLLAR MARRIAGES miniseries has particularly been fun, because Jasper is so delightfully devious. Hope you enjoy *Blind-Date Bride!*

Books by Lori Herter

Silhouette Yours Truly

Listen Up, Lover
*How Much Is That Couple in the Window?
*Blind-Date Bride

Silhouette Romance

Loving Deception #344

Silhouette Shadows

The Willow File #28

Silhouette Books

Silhouette Shadows Short Story Collection 1993
"The Phantom of Chicago"

*Million-Dollar Marriages

1

I hereby bequeath to my beloved wife, Beatrice, fifty percent of my accumulated wealth. To my children, I hereby bequeath the remainder of my estate, to be equally divided among them, on one condition. Each child must marry and remain married to the same spouse for a minimum of one year before he or she can inherit. Failure to marry and remain married for one year will cause the child to be disinherited....

Jasper Derring perused the new clause he had asked his lawyer to add to his will. The newly typed and dated will had arrived in the mail. He took the document into the sunroom of his Chicago lakefront mansion, where his wife of over forty years, Beatrice, was sorting socks.

Jasper began to feel cross, and he didn't know the reason. "Why don't you let Mabel do that?" he said with irritation, referring to their longtime housekeeper. He sat down in a wicker chair across from his wife, who sat on the end of a wicker couch, neatly spreading his dress socks over the flowered cushions.

"I find it reassuring." Wry amusement flickered in Beatrice's hazel eyes as she glanced up at him. Her shoulder-length, gray-white hair was pulled back with a ribbon, George Washington style.

"Sorting socks is reassuring?" he snapped.

"If I can still tell navy from black, I know my eyes are holding up. Small things like that are reassuring when one has edged past sixty-five and is dashing headlong toward seventy," she said, and went on calmly sorting. "What's got you in a snit?"

Not inclined to deal with her question, he tried to sound more nonchalant. "The new will just came from the lawyer."

"Oh."

"So, the new clause is there, just as we discussed, in black and white."

"All legal schmegal?" she said, as if half-interested.

"Yes. No money unless they marry. That's how it is now, whether they like it or not."

"Or whether I like it or not," Beatrice murmured, putting her forefinger through a hole she'd found in the toe of one sock. She put that sock and its mate aside.

"Now, Bea, we discussed this."

"You discussed. I listened."

"You agreed."

"I acquiesced. There's a difference."

"I did what I felt was best for our kids."

"I know," Beatrice said. "And when you know best, no one else knows anything—that is, until you come to a new understanding of what's best. I assumed you'd come to your senses eventually, so rather than cause you to get your dander up, I acquiesced. I don't want you having another heart attack. I only hope you stay healthy long enough to realize you've done a stupid thing. I hope you'll delete that clause, and soon. If you die on us tomorrow, that's the legacy you'll leave our children. I'd ponder on that now and then, Jasper."

He sat straighter in his chair and took on a pontifical tone. "Marriage brings maturity and stability to a young person—qualities our stubbornly single children need to acquire before they can responsibly handle the fortune they stand to inherit. All I want to do is to force them to think seriously about marriage instead of avoiding the issue. Look at Jake, for example—last time we spoke to him he was talking about going off to Antarctica. Last year he was in India, studying the monsoons. He ought to at least start *thinking* of settling down and marrying. He's twenty-nine. He'll be *thirty* in a few months.''

''So old,'' Beatrice said with dry humor.

''Yes, and he's our *youngest son!* He's apparently got no women in his life. Zero. Too busy traveling or teaching at his university. At least our other kids seem to take an interest in the opposite sex.''

''Oh, I'd say one or two are *very* interested in sex,'' Beatrice quipped. ''And they aren't any more inclined to settle down than Jake is.''

''Well, at least Charles has set a good example. He finally got married.''

''With a big behind-the-scenes push from you,'' Beatrice said.

''I saw my chance to move things along and it worked.'' Jasper had enjoyed playing matchmaker for his son. ''And Charles and Jenny have produced our first grandchild.''

Beatrice smiled and set aside the remaining socks. ''I'm as thrilled about little Leslie Ann as you are. And I know that's the real reason behind this change in your will. You want to see more grandchildren before you depart this life.''

''What if I do? Isn't that normal?''

''Very normal. But most prospective grandparents don't threaten their children with disinheritance to make them marry and procreate.''

Jasper shrugged. ''Maybe my methods are…different than the average person's. I've always been one to *make* things happen, not wait for them to happen. I became a multimillionaire by giving people incentives and keeping things moving along.''

"You shouldn't equate interfering in your children's lives with business.''

"I'm not interfering,'' Jasper objected, rising out of his chair. "I'm simply setting parameters for them!''

"Shh,'' Beatrice said. "Sit down. No need to get upset. Relax and work on your needlepoint for a while.''

Jasper sat down and reached for the quilted bag containing his current needlepoint project, a canvas for a pillow meant to commemorate a wedding. It portrayed a heart of flowers with a space inside the heart intended for names and a date to be stitched. There was no date as yet, but Jasper had been working on the names.

He'd taken up needlepoint after his heart attack, to keep him occupied while he was recovering. He'd discovered it to be a very relaxing pastime. But as he looked at his current work-in-progress, he realized its therapeutic benefits wouldn't help just now, and he quickly slipped the project back into the cloth bag. He didn't want Bea to see what he was stitching.

Bea observed him shoving his needlepoint aside. "I'm not going to argue with you,'' she told him in a soothing tone. "I merely have a different point of view. As I told you before, it's your money, you earned it, and I leave it to you to do what you choose with it.''

"You're my life partner, Bea. It's your money, too.''

"When I married you, you were poor. I married *you*, not your bank account. Of course I've enjoyed our beautiful home, the lovely clothes I can afford to buy, the fact that we could send our kids to the best schools. But making and using wealth is your sphere of knowledge, and I give you leave to do as you wish. I trust that in the long run, you'll do the right thing.'' She looked as if she were going to add something, but didn't.

"If I live long enough." With dour humor, Jasper said what she hadn't. "So you think someday I'm going to 'come to my senses' and remove the marriage stipulation?"

"I think so." She nodded. "I may be wrong. But in the forty-some years I've known you, common sense usually prevailed. Sometimes it took years before you realized what the common-sense thing to do was, but eventually you recognized it."

Jasper shifted in his seat, still feeling as uncomfortable and out of sorts as he had when he'd entered the room. Beatrice was usually right about things like this, about family and relationships. But he didn't feel like admitting it to his wife just now. He still wanted to believe his view on the matter had validity.

"Well then, we'll see," he said. "It'll be interesting to observe what reaction I get from each of the kids when I inform them."

"It surely will," Bea said, raising her delicate eyebrows whimsically.

"Why? How do *you* think they'll react?"

"I'm not sure. Except for Jake. I think Jake will tell you what you can do with your new clause. Remember, he doesn't approve of affluence. Jake is embarrassed about his family's wealth."

"He might think differently when he finds out he won't have it anymore unless he gets himself a wife," Jasper said, feeling positive about this, at least. "It's all fine and well to eschew wealth when you've got it at your fingertips if you ever need it. Take it away and see what he thinks."

Beatrice merely shook her head. "You never did understand Jake."

Jake Derring was home in his small condo near the University of Wisconsin campus in Madison, engrossed in creating a final exam for his meteorology students, when the phone rang. He reached for the receiver at the corner of his desk. Instantly he recognized his father's voice.

"Dad! How are things in Chicago? The snowstorm hit you hard?"

"We got a few inches, but it's clear today."

"Still cold, though," Jake warned. "Bundle up good if you have to go out and don't stay outside long. The wind-chill factor can give you hypothermia if you aren't careful."

"Who's the parent here, you or me?" Jasper rasped.

Jake chuckled. Since his father had had a bad heart attack a year and a half ago, the family tended to treat him like an invalid child. "Sorry. I know Mom's taking good care of you."

"As if I can't figure out when to put on a wool coat and scarf myself," Jasper said.

"We just want to keep you healthy," Jake told him. "Don't mean to insult your intelligence, Dad."

"If you want someone to baby, why don't you get married and have a kid of your own?"

Jake half closed his eyes with patience. "Maybe someday I'll do that."

"I hope so, because that's the reason I'm calling. I'm contacting all you kids about a change I made in my will."

Jake drew his brows together. What was this all about? "A change?"

"I'm going to read you a new clause I had the lawyer insert."

Jake listened as his father read. As the gist of the legalese became clear, Jake leaned back in his swivel chair and exhaled with silent impatience.

"You understand what that means?" Jasper asked, when he'd finished reading.

"I think so. If I stay single, I don't get my share," Jake replied, spinning the globe of the earth on his desk.

"That's it."

Jake said nothing, allowing a hollow silence on the long-distance call.

Finally, Jasper said, "Well, you have any reaction to that?"

"No."

"What do you mean, 'no'?"

"I mean," Jake said with pride and tethered irritation, "that I don't give a damn about money. So you can't use that to bribe me or threaten me into getting married."

"That's a fine attitude!" Jasper said in a huff.

"How have my brothers and sister reacted?"

"The only other one I've called so far is Charles."

"I imagine he was a safe call, since he's already fulfilled the new terms by being married for a year," Jake said with sardonic humor. "What did he say?"

"He made some comment that he thought I'd gone too far," Jasper replied in a snappish tone.

"I imagine that's what the others will say, too."

"We're talking about you now."

"Dad, the clauses in your will may come and go, but I will stay the same. I was planning to give ninety percent of my share to environmental research. So, depriving me because I'm not married will only deprive the world of future scientific knowledge. I hope that helps you sleep at night."

"Look at it this way," Jasper said. "If you find yourself a wife, then you'll *have* that money to donate to science. And the ten percent you keep will still give you over a million for your children. Won't that make *you* sleep better?"

Jake looked up at the ceiling. His dad was always clever at turning things around to further his ends. "Why is it so important that we all be married?"

"Marriage is a stabilizing institution. I want my children to acquire some maturity, so they'll use their inheritances wisely."

"I think you just want more grandchildren."

Jasper's voice grew stately and authoritative. "My ticker is not what it used to be. I want to know that my children are settled and secure before I go. It makes me uneasy that all of you—except for Charles—are still so carefree, aimless and single."

Jake grew incensed. There was no way he was going to let himself be characterized as carefree and aimless, no matter how fragile his father's health. "While you're worrying about what'll happen to your money, I'm worrying about what's happening to the earth's atmosphere. My aim is to do all I can to contribute to the research on the ozone layer and the greenhouse effect. There's a lot more happening on this planet to be concerned about than who's married and who stands to inherit the Derring millions!"

"Do you always have to put things in such grandiose terms?" Jasper retorted.

"I'm putting things in perspective. Studying the earth is a major science project," Jake said with sarcastic understatement.

"Don't you ever worry about yourself?"

"I'm happy doing what I'm doing."

"Aren't you ever lonely?"

"I don't have time to be lonely," Jake said, annoyed with the question. "When this semester ends, I'm going down to Antarctica. I'm one of a team of scientists going up in a plane specially equipped to measure trace atmospheric gases, to monitor the hole in the ozone layer."

"Great," Jasper said. "Are any of these scientists women?"

Jake exhaled. "I don't know. I don't think so."

"Don't you like women?"

"Sure, I like women!" Jake said. "But there are more important things I need to be pursuing, especially now while I'm young and have the physical capability to handle harsh climates and strenuous projects. I can still get married and have kids when I'm fifty."

"Fifty?" There was a long pause. "I won't be around to attend your wedding." Jasper's voice sounded sad and elderly now.

A pang of emotion crept into Jake's chest. "I'm sorry, Dad, but I can't plan my life around your desires. I have to do what I have to do."

"So, saving the planet is more important than making your old man happy before he dies?"

Jake set his elbow on the desk and cradled his forehead in his hand. "Do you have to put it that way?"

"I've tried every other tactic with you," Jasper said. "Guilt is my last resort. Can't you be married and still do all the things you want to do?"

"A wife would get in the way, Dad. Women expect attention. Besides, looking for a wife is just too time consuming. It sometimes takes several dates just to find out if a female is interested in me for myself or because I'm a millionaire's son. And even if I managed to find one who isn't after money, who could put up with my peripatetic life, then it would still take months, maybe years, to find out if we're compatible. I don't want to be distracted with all that. And I don't need another major obligation in my life. I'm already dedicated to my students here at the university and to the commitments I've made in the international scientific community to further atmospheric studies. How am I supposed to sort through eligible females with everything else I'm do-ing?''

Jake raked his fingers through his black hair, trying to find enough words to convey to his father the importance of his life's pursuits, wondering if any argument could have much effect on his single-minded parent. He gave up and tried for a lighter approach.

''Let's put it this way, Dad. If you want me to be married, then *you* find me a wife. I don't have the time!''

Silence hung over the telephone line for a full second. Almost hearing the whir of his father's brain working, Jake got an uneasy feeling that he never should have made that quip. At Charles's wedding reception, Jake remembered his brother telling how their father had gone to extreme lengths to play matchmaker. He'd even locked Charles and Jenny overnight together in the family's Chicago department store, hoping sparks between them would ignite. Apparently they had. Jake reassured himself that, up here in Wisconsin, he was out of Jasper's reach.

''Sounds like a good challenge,'' Jasper said, breaking the silence, his tone curiously young and optimistic.

''Dad, I meant that as a joke, to try to show you how impossible my situation would be—''

''Nothing's impossible if one puts his mind to it,'' Jasper said. ''You go on worrying about patching the ozone holes and I'll worry about finding you a wife. I think that's a nice compromise between us.''

''Dad—I was just *kidding!*''

Jasper chuckled. ''I know. Don't give it another thought, Son. When are you going to Antarctica?''

''Next week.''

''For how long?''

''Two weeks.''

''Good. Well, take care *you* don't get hypothermia. And watch out for those polar bears.''

"The bears are up north in the Arctic, Dad."

"Oh. What have they got where you're going?"

"Penguins."

"Perfect. I like penguins. Always look like they're dressed for a wedding! Have a nice trip and give me a call when you get back."

"Sure I will, but—" Before Jake could admonish him again that he was just kidding, his father had hung up. Jake hung up his own phone and closed his eyes. "Stupid! Why did I *say* that?"

In a few moments, he opened his eyes and leaned back in his chair. Maybe he was overreacting. His father would be making calls to the rest of the family and no doubt getting a lot of unpleasant feedback about the clause in his will. By the time he'd gone through all that with all of them, he'd forget about Jake's rash, joking offer. Besides, where would his dad ever find a wife for him, anyway? What young women did Jasper Derring know other than Chicago debutante types, who wouldn't be bothered with a meteorologist up in Wisconsin? Even the logistics of arranging a first date would present difficulties.

Jake began to laugh at himself for getting into such a dither. The whole idea was just too preposterous.

"Want to go out for dinner, Bea?" Jasper asked eagerly, hurrying into the sunroom when he got off the phone.

"Sure," Bea said, looking surprised. "How did your call to Jake go?"

"Great."

Bea looked even more surprised. She blinked. "It did?"

"Jake said *I* should find him a wife."

"What?"

Jasper raised two fingers. "Scout's honor."

Bea squinted at him. "I have the feeling there's more to this than you've told me so far."

He gave her a summary of the entire conversation.

"Then Jake was just making a joke," she surmised.

"Yes." Jasper winked at her. "Why should that stop me?"

"Jasper!"

"I found a wife for Charles, didn't I?" He rubbed his hands together with relish. "This'll be a tougher challenge, but I'm up to it."

"Jasper, you can't be serious. What makes you think... How can you imagine Jake will... Jake is not easygoing like Charles, you know!"

"I'll cross that mountain when I come to it. First I have to secure a wife for him. That's why I want to go out for dinner—how about pizza at Tucci's?"

Bea appeared amused despite herself. Crinkles appeared around her eyes, though she seemed to be trying to keep her mouth from giving in to a smile. "Pizza? I take it this is a clue?"

Jasper nodded.

"If you're thinking of that waitress, Cheri—"

"You've got it!"

"But, Jasper—"

"I know she's not educated like Jake, but she's got spirit and energy and a good heart. It's sweet the way she calls me Mr. Jasper. And she always goes out of her way to special order me a pizza that fits my diet. I can picture her and Jake together as a couple, just like I could Charles and Jenny."

"But, Jasper—"

He raised his forefinger in admonishment. "Don't you say she's not good enough because she's a waitress. I want my sons to marry women who know the meaning of hard work and the value of money."

"I agree," Bea said. "But when we were there last, Cheri mentioned she was planning to marry someone. Remember?"

The reminder hit Jasper like a dump truck. "You're right, she did. Damn!" He'd actually forgotten that. Leaning against the door frame, he bowed his head, momentarily defeated. He had disliked hearing her talk about her new fiancé so much that he'd put it out of his mind afterward, pretended she hadn't said it, not wanting to give her plans even the smallest zap of positive energy by thinking about them.

Jasper looked up. "Had she set a wedding date?"

Bea pondered the question. "It seems to me she said she and her fiancé were preoccupied with going into business and opening a café together. They hadn't gotten around to actual wedding plans yet."

Jasper nodded, remembering. "I had a bad feeling she was getting in over her head. I thought about warning her, but...I didn't." He rubbed his chin as he recalled more details. "I couldn't. She got busy waiting on that big group that came in...." He smiled to himself and murmured, "Maybe fate is at work here. I did start needlepointing her name next to Jake's."

"Needlepointing? Her *name?* Is that what you said?"

Jasper lowered his eyes, self-conscious that he had let that slip. He never could keep anything from Bea for long.

Bea looked askance. "Are you needlepointing another *wedding* pillow? Like the one you made for Charles and Jenny before you threw them together?"

Jasper lifted his hands, palms out. "I needed to start a new project after I finished the nursery pillows for Leslie Ann." He'd become a stitchaholic since he'd become semi-retired due to his health. For him, needlepoint had evolved into a form of cosmic meditation.

"So that's what you've been stitching that you won't let me see. Here I thought it was something for our anniversary! Jasper, just because Charles and Jenny happened to marry, it doesn't mean that every couple you stitch a pillow for will actually *get* married."

"It's the positive thought I put into each stitch, Bea." Jasper refused to even acknowledge her negativity, so it wouldn't enter his mind-set through osmosis. "It brings the idea of a happy union between two particular people into being in the universe. I let God do the rest—with a little help from me, when needed."

"I haven't wanted to tell you this," Beatrice said, "but people say you're growing eccentric. *I'm* beginning to believe them!"

Jasper looked at his wife. "Never take gossip seriously, my dear. It'll warp your mind." He breathed in with zest and lifted his shoulders in a positive stance of good health and good humor. "Well, what do you say? It's been a few weeks since we've been to Tucci's. Why don't we go over and see how Cheri's doing?"

"Now, Jasper, if she's getting married, don't think about breaking up her romance so you can—"

"No, no, I promise I won't go that far," he answered her, raising his right hand as if swearing in court. "But I want to make sure she still *is* getting married. If not, she'd be perfect for Jake."

Bea shook her head with amused resignation. "How do you know?"

"Well, for one thing, her last name is Weatherwax. Shouldn't a woman with that for a name be married to a meteorologist?"

2

At Tucci's Pizzeria, located a block off of Rush Street on the Near North Side, Cheri Weatherwax tried to look perky and pleasant as she carried a deep-dish Chicago-style pizza out of the kitchen. Her bank account was empty and her whole life had gone awry. She didn't have much to be perky about. Right now this job was all she had, so she smiled for her customers and tried to be happy that at least she was working.

With hot pads, she set the round black pan on her customers' table, then brushed back a stray wisp of light brown hair from her eyes. Her shoulder-length hair was caught up in the back with a long, vertical clip. As she used a heavy metal spatula to serve large wedges of cut pizza to the table of four, all men in their twenties, she felt their eyes on her.

Cheri had the sort of voluptuous figure other women envied, yet she wished her body was as straight as a reed. She typically wore oversize sweatshirts to hide her curves. Unfortunately, the waitress's apron tied around her waist hinted at the hourglass shape hidden beneath. She hated the way the men stared at her, yet had dealt with ogling looks enough times in her life to have developed a way to deal with them.

"Nice serve," one of them said with admiration when she set his slice in front of him.

"Thanks."

"What else do you do well?" he asked with a slow, sly grin.

She had a standard answer. "The Heimlich maneuver."

"Do you give demonstrations?" another of the men asked, eyes bright.

"You'd have to be choking first," she said. "I can shove the pizza down your throat, and then give you a demonstration."

The guys laughed.

"How about some more beer instead?" one of them said.

"Sure thing," she replied, and hurried away. As she headed toward the bar, she saw Sam, the thirtyish, dark-haired restaurant manager, leading an older couple to a quiet table in the corner. The man wore a tweed hat with a feather in it. She smiled as she recognized her favorite customers, Mr. Jasper and his wife, Bea. Cheri liked them because they were always friendly and they treated her like a human being. Mr. Jasper's dark eyes were full of inquisitive energy, but he never gave her body the once-over the way most men did. His gray-white hair lent him a stately quality, though he wasn't very tall. He seemed to be retired and had mentioned he'd had a heart attack. His wife was as tall as he, with a slim and elegant figure. He helped her off with her coat. As usual, she was tastefully dressed in a classic white blouse and calf-length skirt.

"I'll take this table, Sam," Cheri said, coming up to the booth where the manager had seated them.

"That would be perfect," Mr. Jasper said as Bea smiled her warm smile.

"Okay," Sam agreed, handing them menus before walking off. "Have a nice dinner."

"Hi! Haven't seen you for a while," Cheri said to the couple. "Has the winter weather kept you away?"

"We do tend to stay in more if it's snowing or very cold," Bea told her. "But Jasper insisted we come here tonight."

Cheri was never sure if Jasper was the gentlemen's first name or his last. His wife called him that, and he had told Cheri she should call him that. But it seemed odd for a first name, and she wondered if he was one of those people whom everyone called by their last name. To be safe, Cheri always addressed him as Mr. Jasper, which, she'd noticed, he seemed to enjoy.

"I'm really glad to see you," she said. "Do you want to look over the menu, or should I just order your usual?"

"The usual for me, if the cook doesn't mind," Jasper told her.

"I'll twist his arm," Cheri said. In shorthand, she scribbled the specifics on her order pad: no mozzarella, no sausage, hold the hot pepper, extra fresh tomato and mushrooms. "And the Chicago Special for you, Bea?"

"Yes. And two salads and herb tea."

"Okay," Cheri said, writing everything down.

"Are you still going into the restaurant business yourself?" Jasper asked.

Cheri managed a grim smile. "No. That . . . sort of fell through."

His brown, almost black, eyes searched hers. "I'm sorry if I've brought up an unhappy subject."

Cheri laughed. "No need to be sorry. My whole life is an unhappy subject."

"Oh, dear. And . . . what about your wedding plans?"

"Up in smoke, too." Cheri was surprised to see a bright new gleam in his dark eyes. She almost detected a hint of glee.

"I had the feeling, when you told us your plans, that you were getting into a situation that might have an unfortunate conclusion," he told her, his tone full of sympathy. "Did the young man turn out to be unreliable?"

"Unreliable is a polite way to put it," Cheri replied. "He suggested, to make it easier to write checks while we were getting our restaurant started, that we open a joint bank account. We were engaged. I trusted him, so I agreed."

"Oh, no!" Bea and Jasper exclaimed in unison.

"'Fraid so. Stupid, huh? Yesterday I went to the bank to make a withdrawal and they told me it had been cleaned out—by my fiancé. He's disappeared and, obviously, I don't expect to hear from him. I'm broke. My dream of opening my own café is down the tubes. I have to start from scratch again."

"What made you trust him?" Bea asked. "You were in love?"

Cheri tapped her order pad on the table, pulling her emotions together so she could talk without her voice breaking. "He seemed different. I'm used to men hitting on me, coming on to me. You can probably guess why. In high school, the guys even wrote untrue graffiti about me on the walls of the boys' rest room."

Bea looked a bit shocked, and her husband shook his head with genuine dismay.

"Believe me, I did nothing to deserve it. I'm not that kind of girl. After the graffiti thing happened, I kept to myself and wore dumpy, loose clothing. My self-esteem sank. Ideas about going to college went out the window, because my grades sank, too. I've toughened up since, but I guess I still wasn't experienced enough to realize that just because a man behaves like a gentleman, it doesn't mean he won't somehow take advantage of you."

"He seemed to treat you with respect?" Bea asked.

"Yeah," Cheri said with a long sigh. "First guy I ever met who never tried anything more than a kiss. He even agreed to wait until we were married to…you know. That was my test for men. If I told them I was waiting for my wedding night, and they still stuck around after I'd made that clear, then I figured they might be worthwhile. He was the first one willing to wait—and I fell for him. I found out too late that what he was really waiting for was my life savings. Fifteen thousand dollars I'd saved since high school, sometimes working two jobs at a time."

"That's awful," Bea said. "Have you no legal recourse?"

"I don't think so. I willingly opened the account with him. He put in money of his own. We managed to get a bank loan. Just as we were to sign papers to buy out a little restaurant in the suburbs, he skipped town with all our account money. I have no idea where he is, and I don't have the funds to hire a detective or a lawyer to go after him. I just want to forget it all."

"So what will you do now?" Jasper asked.

Cheri shrugged. "Hope I win a million in the state lottery! I won't put my faith in people anymore—at least not men." She grinned at the gray-haired man. "Present company excepted. Well, I've got to go and put your order in. I'll be back."

As she hurried across the restaurant, increasingly crowded as the dinner hour approached, she passed the group of four young men she'd served earlier.

"Hey, babe, what about that beer?"

She'd forgotten. But she didn't like being called "babe." "Oh, you wanted that *today?*"

"Think you can manage it?"

Cheri went to the bar, brought them four more beers, then headed for the kitchen. She used her charm, flirting a bit with the cook, to get him to make the special pizza for Jasper, which wasn't on the menu. Once in a while, being a curvaceous female proved to be an advantage, but the bad outweighed the good most of the time.

She made two salads with lemon wedges instead of dressing, as Bea and Jasper always requested, and brought them to their table. She also brought a pot of herb tea.

"I'm so sorry that happened to you," Bea said, sadness in her eyes as Cheri set the teapot on the table.

"I appreciate your sympathy," Cheri said. "I haven't told too many people about it. I don't have a family to confide in, and if I told some of my co-workers here, I'm afraid they'd just laugh at my being so gullible."

"You mentioned winning the lottery," Jasper said.

"Yeah—like with my luck, I would!" Cheri laughed dryly.

"Well," he said with a little tap on her hand as she placed a cup in front of him, "I may be in a position to help you change your luck."

Cheri tucked in her chin as she gazed at him doubtfully. "How?"

"First of all, let me tell you who I am. The first time we came here a few months ago, I told you my name was Jasper. My last name is Derring. Is that familiar?"

Cheri thought a moment. "There's Derring Brothers Department Store on Michigan Avenue."

"Yes! My brother and I founded it together forty years ago. My son Charles took it over when I retired—though I'm chairman of the board. And I oversee the rest of the family's investments, which are numerous, so I'm not completely retired."

A number of thoughts flooded Cheri's mind. He'd founded Derring Brothers? The department store had become a chain, with stores in many of the suburban malls in the Chicago area. Jasper Derring must be . . . incredibly wealthy. Cheri began to feel uneasy, viewing the unobtrusive, friendly couple she'd come to know in a new light.

She nodded slowly. "I see. I never realized I was waiting on such prominent people," she said with embarrassment.

"Oh, don't be silly, Cheri," Bea said. "We brush our teeth, comb our hair and eat pizza just like everyone else. Don't be intimidated. And just go on calling us Bea and Jasper."

Cheri laughed nervously. "Okay, I'll try."

"Bea is right," Jasper said. "But I'm afraid you may be a little bowled over by what I'm going to say next. Would you like to sit down?" He pointed to the empty seat next to Bea.

"Oh, I can't. I don't think my manager would approve. And I have to wait on another table—"

"They can wait a bit more. I'm in a position to help you."

"Like loan me money? Thank you, but with my track record I'm probably not a good risk."

"Not a loan. I have a bargain to strike with you. It's worth a million dollars to you, if you agree. And you won't have to buy any lottery tickets."

"A million dollars?" Stunned, Cheri sank down on the seat next to Bea. "What do you mean, a bargain?"

"The million would be in exchange for a marriage of convenience to my son."

"Marriage of convenience?" she repeated, not quite understanding what that meant. "To the son that runs the department store?"

"No, another son. His name's Jake. He's a meteorologist."

"A weatherman?" she said. "Like on TV?"

"No. A scientist. He teaches at the University of Wisconsin and researches the atmosphere."

Cheri nodded slowly, feeling totally confused. "So what's the marriage-of-convenience part?"

Jasper stroked his nose with his forefinger. "You see, I did something that perhaps I shouldn't have—at least my wife thinks I shouldn't have." He paused to smile at Bea, who was inhaling, as if bracing herself. "I inserted a new clause in my will, stating that each of our children must be married for at least a year, to one person, before they can inherit their share of the Derring fortune. Maybe it was my precarious health and..." he paused, giving Bea an acknowledging glance "...the desire to see more grandchildren that caused me to add such a drastic stipulation. Perhaps I was wrong, but I want to test it before I change my will back again, just in case I'm on the right track, after all."

None of this was making much sense to Cheri, but she went on listening, engrossed by the story he was telling.

"Our son, Jake," Jasper continued, "claims he's too busy to bother to even look for a wife. I think I have a way to—to urge him into the state of matrimony, by making a pact between him, me and you."

"A pact?" Cheri repeated, breathless with anxiety.

"Yes," Jasper replied. "It's rather simple, really. I own an island in Puget Sound."

"Puget...? Where's that?"

"On the West Coast, near Seattle, Washington. There's a house on the island—a little rustic, but charming and livable. I'm planning to have my son spend a year there doing research. I also want him to spend that year being married to you. If you stay married to him for the full year, fulfilling the bargain between us, then I will give you a million dollars. When the year is over, if you don't wish to continue the marriage, then I'll arrange for and pay for a divorce. You get the money in either case."

Cheri rubbed her eyes. "Why should he go along with this idea? Your son, Jake."

"I'm hoping he'll see it as a way to fulfill the stipulation in my will. He'll have the opportunity to try marriage, and even if it doesn't work, he can inherit, just as you will get your million dollars from me."

"This sounds a little crazy," Cheri said. Rich people certainly did things differently than the people she was used to!

"I can understand why you would say that," Bea stated. "I think it's a little crazy, too. But Jasper is rather sure about the proposition."

Cheri felt relieved that Bea agreed with her. Apparently she deferred to Jasper's judgment, however. "You think your son would actually go along with this idea?"

Jasper lifted his shoulders. "I don't know. I haven't discussed it with him yet. I wanted to find out first if you would be willing. I imagine, initially, he'll have the same reaction you're having now—he'll think it's a little crazy. Though he *did* tell me that if I wanted him to be married, *I* should find him a wife. He shouldn't be surprised that I've got a prospective mate for him. It's the year on the island that may bother him."

The word *mate* gave Cheri pause. "Is a marriage of convenience a normal marriage? I mean, do the husband and wife . . . ?"

"You're wondering about the conjugal aspect. That, my dear, is beyond my realm of influence—"

"Thank God," Bea murmured.

Jasper seemed to ignore his wife's comment. "What you do together would be between you and him."

A new thought crept into Cheri's mind, one that might help to explain all this. "Is Jake . . . well . . . gay?"

Jasper shook his head. "No, I don't think so. He's just gotten comatose. He's so focused on his work that playing the mating game gets in his way. He's a dedicated scientist more interested in atmospheric lightning than in creating sparks of his own."

"Well, if I go along with this, marry him, and nothing happens between us, then you're not going to get the grandchildren you're after." Cheri wondered if he'd thought his idea through.

Jasper seemed a bit taken aback. "Yes, I realize that," he acknowledged. "But at least Jake will have tried living with a woman, and he'll qualify himself to inherit. Despite my stringent stipulation, I do want each of my children to inherit their share. At the moment Jake seems the least likely to *ever* marry, and I want him to go through the process, even if it's in name only. It will be a learning experience for him and a way for you to have all the money you need to start your life over again."

Cheri had to admit that the last part sounded enormously appealing, even downright tempting. But it was all too far-out, too wild an idea to consider seriously. Marry someone she'd never even seen? Live on what sounded like a remote island with the guy? For a whole year?

"It's an interesting idea," she said, slowly shaking her head, "and thanks for the offer, but—"

Jasper raised his forefinger. "Now, don't say no yet. Take your time. You don't have to give me an answer tonight. Go over it in your mind. Think of more questions to ask me. I'll give you my personal phone number, so you can call me anytime. This is very important to me. I'm getting to be an old man, so indulge me, please. Give it some serious thought. Remember, your empty bank account, one year from now, could have a million dollars in it. You could open that café you spoke of with no problem. You could be your own boss."

God, he knew all the right words to create an offer she'd have a hard time refusing, Cheri thought. That was exactly what she wanted—to be an independent single woman, running her own successful business, with no man around to mess up her life ever again. A million dollars would certainly set her up forever.

But first she'd have to live with this Jake for a year, and that was the fly in the ointment.

"What do you think your son would expect of me, while we're on the island?" she asked.

"Probably to not bother him too much," Jasper replied.

That certainly sounded ideal, she thought. If it could be a platonic marriage, then maybe it wouldn't be so bad.

All at once the manager caught her eye and gave her a telling look. Instantly she got up from the booth. "I have to get to work," she told Jasper and Bea. "I'll be back when your pizza is ready."

"Fine," Jasper said. "No hurry."

She stopped at the table of young men and absent-mindedly began clearing away their dishes. "Any dessert?"

"What are you offering?" one of them asked in a suggestive tone. The beer had made them more relaxed.

"Mud pie or mud in your eye," she said, annoyed. She was too preoccupied to be bothered with their banter.

"Testy, testy," one of them said.

The manager, who seemed to be keeping an eye on her now, came over. "Is there a problem?"

"They've just got ideas about dessert that aren't on the menu," she explained, trying to make her voice light with humor.

Sam did not seem amused. "What can we get you?" he asked the men. "Mud pie? Key lime pie?"

"Nothing," one of them said, getting out his wallet. "We'll go somewhere else where the atmosphere's more cordial."

Angry now, Cheri walked away with the dirty dishes. When she'd deposited them in the kitchen, she came back out, running into Sam.

"What did you say to them?" Sam asked.

"I said we had mud pie or mud in your eye," she told him. "They seemed to think *I* should be on the dessert menu, too."

"You can handle guys like that without being rude."

"They were rude to me," Cheri said. "Maybe I'm tired of putting up with it."

"Don't you have any sense of humor?"

"When a woman is insulted and doesn't like it, why do men always say she has no sense of humor? What's funny about being treated as if I were a pinup instead of a person?"

"Next you're going to give me some mumbo jumbo about sexual harassment," Sam said, peeved. "I've got a restaurant to run. If you can't handle men who've had a beer or two, then you ought to be working somewhere else. Get my drift?"

"Yes," she said.

A new couple had come in and was sitting at a table to which she was assigned. As she walked across the floor to take their order, she happened to glance at the restaurant's front door, which had been accidentally left open. She detoured to the entrance to close it. As she did, she looked out and saw something moving in the snow at the edge of the sidewalk.

"Kitty," she said with dismay. It was a small brown cat, perhaps a half-grown kitten, that had been lingering around Tucci's for the last week or so, looking for food. She and another waitress had started feeding it in the back, outside the kitchen. When the cat saw her, it ran inside, jumping over her feet. Cheri hurried after it. According to law, animals were not permitted in the restaurant.

She picked up the cat, held it protectively against her and hurried through the restaurant toward the kitchen.

Jasper and Bea smiled as they saw her rush by with the animal. Unfortunately, she ran into Sam again.

He eyed the feline with disgust. "I told you not to let that cat hang around here anymore! What's it doing inside?"

"She ran in before I could stop her," Cheri said. "She's just hungry."

"Cheri," Sam said, "I know you've worked here for over three years, but you can't bend the rules to suit yourself. You can't sit with customers, you can't be rude to them and you can't indulge a hungry cat! If you continue this way, you're out of here!"

Tears starting in her eyes, Cheri hurried to the kitchen with the cat, set the animal down just outside the back door and found a small, clean plate. She hunted up some cheese, some cooked hamburger that hadn't been seasoned and some pizza crust. She put it down in front of the green-eyed cat, who meowed and then dove into its supper hungrily. Cheri felt a genuine empathy with the animal. She and the cat were in the same position at the moment, living hand-to-mouth, unsure who their friends were, with almost no one to depend on.

That million dollars Jasper Derring had offered was looking better and better by the second. But she knew she was too upset now to make any decision, and she told herself to follow Jasper's advice and think it over. She composed herself, washed her hands, then went back to work.

A little later, Jasper and Bea's pizzas were ready and she brought them to their table.

Bea seemed to study Cheri's eyes, as if noticing she'd been upset. "Are you all right?"

"Oh, yeah," Cheri assured her. "Just another day around here. Frankly, Jasper's suggestion sounds pretty good at the moment."

The gentlemen's eyes positively lit up.

"But I'm going to think it over, as you told me," Cheri hurried to add.

Jasper smiled. "Of course, of course. But I'm glad, thrilled, that you're willing to consider it. I do understand how odd a proposition it is."

"Can I ask you something?" Cheri said. "Why did you pick me to marry your son for a year? I'm not educated the way he must be. I'm just a waitress—a gullible one at that."

Jasper leaned toward her, his demeanor earnest and sincere. "My dear, you're trusting, not gullible. And you're considerate—you've always been thoughtful toward me, even before you knew who I was. You're honest and genuine. And you want to better yourself through your own efforts, by saving and starting your own business. I admire your ambition. Unfortunately, you had a bad break. But you have a lot of positive energy. I don't know any young woman who would make Jake a better wife."

Tears filled Cheri's eyes. The compliments and affirmation from Jasper were comforting, compared to what she'd gotten from her boss and other customers that day. She blinked the moisture back. "What does Jake look like?"

Jasper relaxed and smiled. "Let's see. He's got black hair. He's taller than me—well, all my sons are. He's nearsighted, so he's often wearing glasses. Always was the studious type."

"Do you have a picture?" she asked. If she was actually going to consider living with a stranger for a year, she ought to at least see what he looked like.

Bea reached for her purse. "I think I do. Wait." She shuffled through her purse and brought out a small photo album. Turning the plastic pages, she opened it flat and handed it to Cheri. "That was taken on his twenty-fifth birthday. He's twenty-nine now. How old are you, Cheri?"

"Twenty-three," Cheri said. While Bea murmured that six years wasn't all that far apart, Cheri studied the photo. She couldn't say Jake looked ugly. His hair was clipped a little shorter than she liked, and the glasses gave him a scholarly quality, but he looked a lot better to her than any of the young boors at the table she'd waited on earlier. And he looked a lot more reliable than her blond, blue-eyed, former fiancé. She'd never trust a smooth-talking Brad Pitt type again, however cute his smile was.

She bit her lip as she carefully gave the photo album back to Bea. "He looks nice enough."

The woman's eyes warmed with pride. "Jake is special. So bright he skipped grades in school, whizzed through college and got his Ph.D. when he was twenty. He's what you'd call a do-gooder, I suppose. He wants to save the world, and he doesn't think much about himself. Very altruistic. You won't find a man like him around every corner."

Cheri smiled a little and leaned toward Bea, pretending to ignore Jasper. "Just between you and me, what do you think about all this? Do you really want me to marry your son?"

Bea smiled. "I wish the circumstances were more normal, that you and he had met and decided on your own to marry. I'm not into matchmaking to the degree that Jasper is. But I'll tell you honestly, Cheri, that I think you'd make a lovely wife for any of my sons."

Cheri swallowed at the high compliment. "Thank you," she said in a whisper.

"Remember, you're only obligated to stay married for a year," Jasper reiterated.

Cheri nodded. "I'll think about it. I really will." She'd probably come to her senses tomorrow, when she was no longer so emotional and upset by events. But Jasper was unbelievably kind, and she was glad that today she could honestly promise him she'd consider his idea.

3

"How was Antarctica?" Dr. Eisler, the head of the Meteorology department, asked with a smile.

"Cold," Jake replied, walking into Dr. Eisler's office. The gray-haired, older man stood, and they shook hands. "Got a lot of data though, so it was worth it."

"Good to have you back. Got some news for you," Dr. Eisler said. "The Summerwind Foundation for Atmospheric Studies, the one that provided the funds for our new computer system last year, is offering our department another grant. This one would be earmarked for a year-long study of the microclimate of the San Juan Islands in Puget Sound."

Puget Sound? Jake thought, growing alert.

"If the study is completed within fourteen months from the date of this letter," Dr. Eisler continued, sitting behind his desk again, "we'd get an additional grant of $500,000 to use as we wish. You've often mentioned you have a special interest in that area, so perhaps you'd be open to being selected to undertake this study."

"You bet I would! This is incredible." Jake grinned and eagerly sat down in the chair in front of Dr. Eisler's desk. "It's like a gift! I've been fascinated by that microclimate ever since I was a teenage weather addict. I traveled there with my dad years ago when he was look-ing into buying one of the smaller islands as an investment. I wanted to know how the climate on the islands can be so dry when they're located in a region that's known for its rain. What a coincidence that they've approached *us* to do this study!''

Suddenly, a new thought sped through Jake's mind, and he began to grow uneasy. Maybe it wasn't a coincidence. He hesitated, then glanced at Dr. Eisler. "Has anyone on our staff looked into this Summerwind Foundation? Do you know where their money comes from? Who decides what projects they'll offer grants for?"

Dr. Eisler lowered his eyes. "It's a relatively new foundation, so it doesn't have a track record to explore." He smiled. "Their money's good—always comes promptly when it's promised—so why look a gift horse in the mouth?"

This vague reply gave Jake pause, and it also added to his suspicion.

Dr. Eisler quickly moved on. "If you do this study, you'd have to take a leave of absence. You were going to take your sabbatical next year, but I think we can bend the rules a bit and let you take it this year. This study might be a feather in your cap and ours if it reveals some significant new data."

"I know." Jake nodded, his stomach tightening. "I'll think it over."

Dr. Eisler seemed puzzled by his change in demeanor. "Don't wait too long to give me your answer. If you decide to go to Puget Sound, arrangements will have to be made for someone else on staff to take over your classes this coming semester."

"Why does this study have to start so quickly?"

Dr. Eisler lifted his hands. "It's what the representative from the foundation requested. Maybe they need the results for some project of their own. It's none of our business, really. They've been good to us in the past, and we could use the $500,000 bonus they're offering. We've been wanting to start a new scholarship program.''

"Yes, I realize that. Let me think it over." Jake said goodbye and walked down the hall to his own office. He went to his window and looked out at the campus buildings of brick and stone.

He couldn't help but wonder if this magnanimous Summerwind Foundation could be the invention of some eccentric millionaire—his father, for example. He wondered if the foundation had a certain island in mind—like the four-mile-square one Jasper had bought years ago. His father had had the idea of turning it into an exclusive resort, but had never followed through. Rather than ask Dr. Eisler any more questions that the department head didn't seem anxious to answer, Jake decided to take a shortcut.

He phoned his father at home. After preliminary greetings, Jake got right to the point.

"Do you have anything to do with the research grant for Puget Sound that my department was offered?''

"You were offered a grant?" Jasper asked innocently.

"Dad, be straight with me. Are you behind the Summerwind Foundation?''

"So you figured it out." Jasper sounded amused over the telephone line.

"It's true then?" Jake exclaimed, surprised despite his suspicions.

"It was your mother's idea initially. She wanted to support you in your career, so she suggested we should give some grants to your department. I set up the Summerwind Foundation for that purpose.''

Jake felt embarrassed. "Does Dr. Eisler know that my father is the source of those funds?''

"He found out when he had the foundation investigated before accepting my first grant. Since then we've had some nice phone conversations. When I suggested the Puget Sound study, I didn't even have to spell out for him that I wanted it directed to you. He and I understand one another. And he's very appreciative of what the foundation has done and still can do for his department."

I can imagine, Jake thought. "Why exactly *did* you decide to give a grant for a meteorologic study of Puget Sound? Are you going to resurrect your idea of building a resort there?"

"No," Jasper replied. "But it's something you've been mentioning you'd like to study ever since you were a kid."

"So you're just trying to make me happy?" Jake asked.

"You could say that."

"I have a feeling there's some catch here."

"You're right, there is," Jasper conceded in a wry tone. "It happens that I may have found you a wife."

"Good Lord," Jake muttered under his breath. "You must be out of your mind!" he exclaimed into the receiver.

"No, not quite," Jasper teased. "Not yet, anyway."

"I told you I was just joking."

"But you shouldn't treat it as a joke, because it was an excellent idea."

"Dad, there's no way under the sun that I'm going to go along with an arranged marriage!"

"Remember, Jake, it would fulfill the new terms of my will. All you have to do is stay married to her for a year."

"This is ridiculous—"

"It can be the same twelve months you spend doing research in Puget Sound. Two birds with one stone, son. No waste of time. You make your contribution to science and earn an additional $500,000 for your department, and you fulfill the stipulation of being married for a year. Then, someday when you inherit your share, you'll have all that money to use or donate to whatever scientific studies you wish. Look at it this way—you'd be doing it for the benefit of mankind."

Jake gazed grimly out the window to the snow-covered campus. It became difficult to argue when his father was offering ways to channel money to causes so close to Jake's heart. "This is bribery. It's invasive—you're trying to control my personal life!"

"Only for a year."

"That's 365 days too many."

"She's a terrific young woman, Jake."

"If she's so terrific, why would she be willing to marry someone she's never met?" Jake asked, trying to use logic, knowing it was probably lost on his father.

"She's had some personal setbacks. And...I offered her a million dollars."

"Ah, now we're getting down to brass tacks," Jake said. "A *million?* I imagine lots of women would be willing to marry any clod for a year for that!"

"That may be true," Jasper conceded. "But she's special. I think you'll find her compatible enough to share a household."

"You mean, she's agreed already?"

"No, not yet. I told her to think about it and she's still doing that. But she's called me to ask questions about the arrangement. I expect a final answer from her soon."

Obviously his father had dug up some gold digger for him to marry. She might strike Jasper as being compatible and "special," but Jake decided the best way out of this would be to expose her for what she was.

He rubbed his forehead, trying to figure out what tack to take. "If I'm supposed to marry this—this woman, why don't you give me her phone number, so I can talk to her? Get to know her a little. That's fair, isn't it, since I'm the one who's supposed to live with her?"

There was silence for a long moment. "All right," Jasper agreed. "She gave me her number. She'd probably like to talk to you, too. Got a pen?"

Jake wrote down the number Jasper read to him. "*Thanks*, Dad," he said with mock appreciation. "I'll call her now."

"No, no, she'll be at work, since it's late afternoon," Jasper said. "I'd call her after 9:00 p.m. Or on Monday. That's her day off."

Jake grew puzzled. "What does she do?"

"She's a waitress."

"A waitress...." The information dumbfounded Jake. His father thought she would be a good match for him? "Dad, what would a waitress and a meteorologist have in common?"

"You both need a little lightning in your lives."

Jake could make a pretty good guess what Jasper meant by that. "And this waitress is going to create sparks?"

"You haven't met her," Jasper said. "I've seen men salivate when she merely pours them a glass of water."

"Really!" Jake was almost amused now. "If she's so desirable, why would she want to marry a stuffy university professor, million dollars or not? She could probably find a millionaire on her own."

"She's not like that," Jasper said. "She's not after money. Not really. She has a good heart."

Jake laughed out loud. "So she's willing to take a million dollars to marry a perfect stranger for altruistic reasons?"

There was another long silence. "Call her on the phone and talk to her. See what impression you get."

The admonition surprised Jake. "All right. I intend to. What's her name?"

"Cheri Weatherwax."

Jake hesitated after he wrote the name. "Is this a joke?"

"No, that's really her name. It's what gave me the clue that she was destined for you."

Jake clenched his jaw, said a curt goodbye and hung up. He didn't want to get into any further conversation about "destiny." The older his father got, the more metaphysical ideas seemed to fascinate him, and the words *fate* and *destiny* had begun to enter his conversation regularly. Someday Jake would point out to his father that if "destiny" were truly at work, why did it need so much help from him?

That evening, Jake sat at home on his couch, his hefty black-and-white cat, Dude, snoozing next to him while he watched CNN. But his mind wasn't on the news. As the hour crept past 9:00 p.m., he kept staring at the phone. Should he call her?

When 9:30 rolled around, he decided he might as well get the chore over with. He dug the number his father had given him out of his wallet. While Dude yawned and stretched, he dialed the phone on the end table next to him.

"Hello?" The high-pitched, feminine voice that answered sounded tired.

"Is this Cheri Weatherwax?"

"Yes."

"My dad gave me your number—Jasper Derring."

"Oh . . . yes. You mean you're—?"

"Jake Derring."

"Jake. They showed me your photo. It's nice to meet you . . . er, talk to you. I'm kind of glad you called."

Jake was a little surprised by her response. She sounded polite and reasonable. It occurred to him that Jasper might be twisting her arm into going along with this proposed marriage, and maybe she didn't know how to refuse such an important man. Perhaps they could agree this whole plan was ridiculous and together give Jasper a firm *no*. "I wanted to know what you think of my father's nutty idea."

She chuckled. "That was my first reaction, too. It was like being asked to be a blind-date bride. I don't know, maybe *I'm* nutty, but more and more I'm tempted to go along with it."

Jake drew his brows together. He didn't like the sound of this. "May I ask why?"

"Of course. I'm glad we have this opportunity to talk. I was going to ask Jasper if I could speak to you." She hesitated, perhaps gathering her thoughts. "I guess the reason this idea is beginning to sound good to me is because my life is in such a mess right now. I lost all my money—or rather, it was stolen."

"Stolen? That's terrible," Jake said, reluctantly sympathetic to her plight.

"My fiancé—former fiancé—and I were going into business together. I opened a joint bank account with him. Put my entire savings into it. A few days later he withdrew it all and disappeared."

Jake listened, a bit less sympathetic now that he'd heard the details. She must not be a very good judge of character, he was thinking. "You were going to marry this guy?"

"Yeah." Her voice grew rueful and a trifle wistful. "He looked like Brad Pitt."

Jake winced. She sounded like a freshman coed. "You may be considering this marriage of convenience because you're on the rebound. I *don't* look like Brad Pitt or any other movie star. I'm a boring college professor. You might rebound into disappointment."

"I know. I saw your photo."

She doesn't have to be so quick to agree, he thought.

"But you don't sound boring," she continued. "Jasper said you just got back from Antarctica, so you must lead a pretty exciting life. And besides, it's not a real marriage. Just for a year, that's what your dad keeps saying. I've decided I don't really want to be married, anyway. I want to go through life single. So it's not a rebound situation at all. The only reason I'm considering it is because it will be only a *temporary* marriage."

"I imagine the million dollars my dad promised you makes the whole idea seem pretty appealing, too," Jake said, deciding to cut to the chase.

There was a brief silence. "Well, I've been arguing with Jasper about that over the phone. When he first said a million dollars, I—I couldn't really believe it. Couldn't take it in. Of course it sounds great, especially to someone who's broke. But the more I thought about it, the more anxiety ridden I got. I'd be afraid of doing the wrong thing and losing all that money, just like I lost my own savings. I told Jasper I'd be happy to get $15,000 for marrying you, since that's the amount I lost. That would put me on my feet again. I—I'd be really afraid to receive a whole million."

Jake found himself slumping. He knew it was illogical, but somehow it came as a blow to his ego that $15,000 was all he was worth in her judgment. He sat up straight and tried to regain some dignity. At least her refusal of the million dollars indicated she wasn't as mercenary as he'd assumed.

"So, you're willing to agree to give up a year of your life for $15,000?" Jake asked with amazement.

"No, I don't look at it that way. I told you, my life is in a shambles. I have no money. I hate my job. I recently adopted a cat that my apartment owner says I can't keep. I'm not sure if I can make the rent, anyway. Nothing's working out. A year away on an island sounds nice, frankly."

Jake found himself wincing again. He was beginning to understand where she was coming from and why this whole preposterous idea apparently appealed to her. He'd hoped she would be appalled.

"I'd been planning to open a small café," she continued. "That was the business venture my fiancé and I were involved in before he ran off with my money. I could use the year away to study up on business. Maybe take a correspondence course or two. I only have a high-school education, so I have a lot to learn. And I could use the time to develop recipes for my café menu. So this island idea is getting harder and harder to pass up. I'd have a year to get my act together, and when the year is up, I'd have money to start my own business."

"You might need a little more than fifteen thousand," Jake said.

"I know. Actually, so far your dad has refused to lower the sum. He keeps insisting that he offered me a million and he intends to honor that." She laughed a bit. "He said that to live with you for a year, I'll have earned a million dollars."

"Did he?" Jake said, trying to sound amused. "Well, you know, he may be right. I'm very focused on my work. I get cranky if I'm interrupted. I'm hopelessly self-absorbed. Like you, I much prefer the single life."

"Well, it's fine with me if we just keep to ourselves and out of each other's way. I'll have lots of studying to do. I'd spend a lot of time in the kitchen, too. We could sort of... you know, each have our own room."

"Don't worry," Jake said with sober humor. "If we did this, we absolutely would have separate rooms."

"So..." She hesitated, then continued, "It would be platonic, right? The marriage of convenience? That's... how I envision it."

"Definitely!" Jake agreed. "But I'm afraid the whole idea doesn't sound as appealing to me as it does to you."

"Oh." She sounded disappointed.

"I don't like the way my father is trying to manipulate me," Jake explained, deciding to be straightforward and honest with her. "He made a grant to my university so I could have a year off to study the microclimate around the island. He's found you to go along with this marriage scheme. If I ever do marry, I want it to be in my own time and to the person of my choice, not because my father has decreed that I *must* marry." There was a touch of anger in his voice.

"I know," she said with empathy. "He explained about the new clause in his will. But he said it's because he really wants you to inherit your share, so he's trying to make it easy for you to fulfill the terms of the will."

Jake pressed his lips together. Jasper had obviously misled her slightly, just as he'd tried to camouflage his real reasons to Jake. "What my dad really wants, Cheri, is for us to fall in love. He's decided, apparently because your last name is Weatherwax, that you'd be the perfect wife for me. I think he's figuring that if we spend a year alone together on an island, things will happen, we'll fall for each other and then we'll *stay* married."

"Ohh..." Her voice trailed off as the light apparently dawned in her mind. "You know, I wondered about that. He mentioned that part of his reason for all this was a desire to see more grandchildren before...well, before he passes on. I've been wondering why Jasper would be satisfied if we stayed married for only a year and then got divorced. It's not a very good arrangement for producing grandchildren. But you think that he figures once we're married, we'll...get to like each other...."

"Exactly," Jake said, glad she was able to absorb this point. She sounded a little too trusting—but rather sweet, he had to admit.

"So he'd be really disappointed if it doesn't turn out that way," she surmised.

"That would be *his* problem," Jake said. "But we'll never find out, because I'm not ready to buy into his matchmaking scheme."

"I see," she said. "I understand. You have your career. It would disrupt your life, your work."

"Not necessarily," Jake reluctantly admitted. "He's come up with a clever inducement. The study he's given a grant for is one I've always wanted to do. I have a sabbatical coming up, too."

"What's that?"

"Every several years, a professor gets a year off to do research, perhaps write a paper for a scientific journal. There's a saying in the academic community: publish or perish."

"I see," she said again, though she didn't sound sure. "So, why do you want to pass up the opportunity?"

"Because it's all a huge manipulation to get me married, and I resent that," he repeated with some testiness.

"Oh, yes, of course." She sighed into the phone. The sound in his ear caused an odd little rush to go through him. "But at least it's nice your father takes this much interest in you and your future," she said, as if trying to reassure him. "My father left my mom and me when I was two. I have no idea where he is. He's never given a damn about me. It sounds like your father is just the opposite—maybe a little too interested. But I'd settle for a dad like that. No one is perfect."

Jake began to feel sad for her. She seemed to be one of those people who had one bad break after another. "What's your mom like?" he asked.

"She died two years ago."

"I'm sorry." God, Jake was thinking, besides being sweet and naive, she's an orphan, too.

"Thanks. It's hard, because she was always the only one who understood me. She really stood up for me in high school when I...had a major problem. I miss her."

Jake was curious, but didn't ask what her problem had been. She had a pleasant voice and an amiable way of expressing herself, but he didn't want to be drawn into her personal situation. Her comments about wishing she had a father more like his were starting to soften him toward her, he realized. She and his parents seemed to have formed a mutual admiration society. Jake almost felt a little left out.

"I guess I saw Jasper's offer as a way to start over again, have a better future," she said. "But it's not that way for you, is it? If you say no, I'll understand."

She sounded so damn sweet. Was she for real? "Do you mean you'd really be willing to live in the same small house with me, an absolute stranger, for a year?" he asked.

"Well, if I have to get a new apartment because of my cat, I may have to find a roommate to help pay the rent. That person would probably be someone I don't know. I'd look upon you the same way—as a . . . a housemate. I'd do the cooking—I'm good at it. And I'd be willing to clean and do laundry. There might be outside chores— your father said the couple there now have a garden. If we decide to keep up the garden, then maybe we could share those tasks. But the rest of the time you'd have free to do your scientific work."

Jake ran his hand over his face. "You almost make this sound like a good arrangement," he said with humor.

"Well, I've had a few weeks to think about it, and the more I have, the more I've realized what an opportunity it is—million dollars or not."

"But we'd still be alone on this island. People can get in each other's way sometimes. And it doesn't seem like you and I have much in common. We have totally different life experiences."

"Being a waitress, I've learned to tolerate lots of different types of people. As long as you behave like a gentleman—and your mom and dad indicate you're nothing but—I won't have any problem with you. You may find some irritating things about me, I suppose. But if you tell me what bothers you, I'll try to change or keep out of your way altogether. We don't even have to eat together, if you don't want to. I can just bring you your meals and leave. I'm good at carrying food on a tray.''

Jake smiled. ''You do make this whole thing sound palatable—sorry, I didn't mean to make a pun.''

She chuckled. ''It would make your father happy, too. He's always so kind and caring. I feel sorry that he had that heart attack.''

Jake said nothing, not wanting guilt about not fulfilling his father's wishes to influence him. But then he thought again. His father's health was definitely poor. Jake didn't like to think about the possiblity that his dad might die unhappy with him. If he went along with this idea, at least his father wouldn't have any more ammunition to use to get him married. He'd also be able to spend a year on a meteorologic study that interested him a great deal. Two birds with one stone, as Jasper had pointed out. And . . . it *would* be nice to have someone around to cook, Jake acknowledged to himself.

''Hello?'' Cheri said, apparently wondering if he was still on the line.

''I'm here,'' he said. ''Just thinking.''

''Is the idea beginning to sound better to you?''

''I'm afraid so,'' he answered, wondering if there was something wrong with him.

''I don't want to talk you into it,'' Cheri said, ''but I hope you'll consider it—and not just for my sake, either. I didn't mean to burden you with a sob story. I was just explaining my side of it. Even if your dad *is* a little scheming, he means well, and it sounds like he's set up a nice opportunity for both of us.''

Jake rubbed his nose. "Okay. I'll give it some more thought."

"Good," she said. "By the way, how was Antarctica?"

He described to her the base where the plane from New Zealand had landed, and the specially equipped aircraft that flew 70,000 feet above the earth, into the stratosphere, to measure trace gases.

"You must be brave," she said. "I'd be scared to do that."

The comment interested him. It seemed to him that she was rather brave living on the edge of bankruptcy as she was and still managing to be so good-natured. Lack of money had never been a problem for Jake, nor had he ever been worried about having a place to live. "You'd handle it okay," he told her. "Handling my father is a greater challenge."

"Oh, Jasper's a teddy bear," she said. "I never even knew he was rich until a few weeks ago. I didn't know his last name was Derring. Your parents just seemed like a homey, down-to-earth couple who came in for pizza every once in a while."

"I used to think Dad was down-to-earth," Jake said. "Lately he seems to be hovering above ground with all the unpredictibility of a UFO. And what's he doing eating pizza? He's supposed to be on a strict diet."

"The first time they came in, he told me he'd have to order a salad. But I said I could ask the cook to leave off the cheese and sausages and add more vegetables. So he always orders that now."

Jake couldn't help but be touched that she apparently went to extra trouble for his dad. No wonder Jasper thought she was special. "That's very nice of you. My dad may exasperate me, but I want to keep him healthy. Well, I'll mull this over some more and call you back. I think it's fair to notify you of my decision before I tell my father.''

''I'll support you, whatever you decide.''

''Thanks for being so understanding,'' he said with appreciation. ''Goodbye.''

Jake hung up and sat still for a moment, feeling a little at sea. His conversation with Cheri had gone amazingly well, for two people who had never met. That alone made him think that maybe this wasn't such a bad idea, after all. They might be quite compatible as *housemates,* the word she'd used. Nevertheless, he intended to sleep on it—for *several* nights.

Three days later, having thought through all the angles until he was sick of the matter, and after enduring eager smiles and questioning looks from Dr. Eisler every day, Jake dialed Cheri's number.

''I've decided to do it,'' he told her, feeling a bit short of breath for some reason. ''That is, if you're still willing.''

''Oh, that's great! Of course I'm willing. This will change my life around. But I really hope it'll be a fruitful year for you, too. And when it's over, we can both just go back to being single again!''

''Right,'' Jake said, wishing he could feel as positive and lighthearted about it as she did. ''Then we're agreed. So, do you want to call my dad, or should I?''

''I imagine he'd rather hear the good news from you,'' she said. ''By the way, can I bring my little cat with me to the island?''

''Sure. I'll be bringing my cat, too. We'll have to hope they get along.''

''You have a cat?'' she asked with surprise. ''What's her name?''

''It's a male. His name's Dude.''

''That's clever,'' she said. ''I'm still deciding what to call mine. It's a stray kitten that kept coming to the restaurant for food. The manager didn't like it, so I took it home with me one night.''

''If they don't like each other, then yours can be an outdoor cat and mine can be indoor. Dude doesn't like to go out. Pretty lazy cat, actually. Sleeps most of the time. He's getting fat.''

She laughed. ''We'll put him on a diet.''

''Good,'' Jake replied, unsure what to say next. ''Okay then! I'm sure we'll be in touch before we...we leave for Puget Sound.'' He nervously said goodbye and hung up, wondering why he was feeling so rattled. He was making everyone happy—Cheri, Dr. Eisler and his father. Maybe his uneasiness was because Jake wasn't sure *he* was going to be happy with this decision. It felt more like a shot in the dark than a scientific research project.

He dialed his father's number. ''Dad? It's Jake. You win.''

''You mean you'll marry Cheri?''

''You seem to have engineered an offer too good for either of us to refuse.''

''Wonderful! I'll begin making all the arrangements.''

''I don't want any big ceremony,'' Jake hastened to tell him. ''I've had a long talk with Cheri. She and I have no intention of staying married. So forget any church nuptials with a reception and a wedding cake and all that jazz.''

''Okay,'' Jasper said. ''How about a small, private ceremony in a judge's chambers?''

''All right, but I want to keep this 'marriage' quiet. Find some judge in Seattle.''

''You've got it!'' Jasper assured him with delight.

4

Cheri had to watch where she stepped as Jasper led her into a room in the Seattle courthouse. A large, paint-spotted cloth covered the carpeting. Another drape covered a desk. The walls were partly repainted; the previous ivory color was being replaced with a pale blue. The windows were wide open and the room felt cold. Cheri zipped up her three-quarter-length winter jacket again.

Jasper had accompanied her from Chicago to Seattle, a city she'd never visited. Bea didn't like to fly, so she'd stayed home. They'd left Cheri's sedated cat at the airport with airline personnel for a few hours.

"Is this the judge's chambers?" she whispered to Jasper with doubt.

Jasper appeared crestfallen as he glanced about the room. All at once, a bald man of about forty-five dressed in an expensive-looking suit walked in.

"Jasper Derring?" he said with a smile.

Jasper turned around. "Judge Akins? Nice to meet you." They shook hands. "Was there a misunderstanding about the date?"

Judge Akins looked only slightly self-conscious. "Sorry. The painters were supposed to come yesterday, and the room would have been finished. But they had a delay, so they're here today. Won't affect the legality of the wedding vows, though," he joked. "Is this the bride?"

Cheri smiled as the judge extended his hand. "Yes, I'm Cheri Weatherwax."

"Not for long!" he said, giving her hand a squeeze before letting it go. "Where's the groom? Unless . . . did I misunderstand? Are you two the happy couple?"

"No," Jasper said, irritably. "My son. His plane was supposed to land only a half hour after ours. We stopped for lunch. I thought he'd be here ahead of us."

"Maybe he's caught in noon-hour traffic," the judge said. "The painters are due back at 1:00 p.m. And I have to be in court at 1:30. Hope he can get here."

"If he doesn't, I'll wring his neck," Jasper muttered.

Cheri looked out the open window. It was raining now. She shivered a bit. This was going to be some wedding day, she thought, aware of the smell of paint fumes. A ladder stood in one corner of the room, and paint cans sat at its base. This wasn't quite what she'd imagined her wedding day would be like.

When she was a little girl, she'd always envisioned herself wearing a white gown and walking down the aisle—alone, since her father was not around to give her away. Then, in high school, when she'd lost her self-esteem, she'd stopped thinking about weddings. When she was engaged to her fiancé, he'd always said he wanted to fly to Las Vegas and get married. She realized now that that was probably so they wouldn't have to make any wedding arrangements ahead of time, since he'd never intended to marry her anyway.

However, when Jasper had told her that he'd arranged to have her married to Jake by a judge in a courthouse, she'd thought that the ceremony, however brief, would be rather formal and serious. She'd even dressed in a white lace blouse with a calf-length gray wool skirt for the occasion. If she'd known what the judge's chambers were going to look like, she would have worn jeans and an old sweatshirt.

Not that it mattered what she wore if the groom didn't show up. She wondered if Jake had changed his mind. Jasper seemed more and more antsy.

A few minutes later a tall, black-haired man wearing glasses came through the door. He glanced at the ladder and the half-painted walls, as if wondering if he was in the right place. His eyes, which were a very deep brown, resembled Jasper's. Cheri recognized him from the photo Bea had shown her, though he looked different somehow. His hair was somewhat longer and slightly wavy. His eyes had a few lines around them and his face wasn't as thin as in the photo. He'd aged a bit—and he'd aged well. Cheri found herself growing surprisingly shy. As Jasper walked forward to greet him, she hung back a bit.

"Where the hell have you been?" Jasper asked him.

"I didn't have a direct flight, and there was a delay in between," Jake said, wiping raindrops off his glasses with the plaid lining of his unbuttoned raincoat. Underneath he wore a black sweater over a shirt and pants. "Then the cab driver had to contend with lunch-hour traffic."

"Just as I thought," the judge said, smiling as he came forward to shake Jake's hand. "I'm Judge Akins. Sorry to rush things, but the painters will be back soon. We have our bride and groom present. Any witnesses?"

"I asked you to provide them," Jasper reminded him. "You must have a clerk, a secretary—"

"At lunch. I forgot about that." As Judge Akins was scratching his head, two men in white, paint-splattered overalls came in. "Luck is with us! The painters are back early. Maybe they'll be willing to be witnesses." He walked to the ladder and spoke with them.

Cheri glanced from Jasper, obviously peeved and impatient, to Jake, who looked baffled by what was going on. He caught her gaze, however, and his expression changed, as if he were just now realizing who she was. He stepped up to her.

"You're Cheri?"

"You're Jake?" she said with a hesitant smile.

Both chuckled self-consciously.

"Things haven't quite worked out the way Jasper planned," Cheri whispered. "The judge seems to have botched things up a little."

Jake shook his head, laughing softly. "I thought about wearing a suit. I'm glad I didn't." He gazed at Cheri, his dark eyes taking in her features.

"Good thing you didn't," she said. "Might have gotten paint on it." While she nervously joked, she wondered what he was thinking about her. Though he was polite and somewhat studious looking, Cheri had the gut feeling that his libido wasn't quite as frozen as Jasper had led her to believe. He certainly wasn't flirting with her or ogling her—with her thick jacket on, there was nothing to ogle—yet he came across as very alive and warm-blooded. The idea of having a husband, of being Jake's wife for a year, suddenly shifted from an abstract idea to something very real. Living with him, even platonically, was going to be an entirely new experience for her.

"It's settled!" Judge Akins proclaimed, walking back to them, followed by the two bashful painters. "We have our witnesses. We have our bride and groom. Now we can have our wedding!"

Cheri chewed her lip as Jasper handed the judge a marriage license. Her and Jake's blood tests had been taken in the Midwest and the results forwarded to Seattle. Each had separately signed the license, which Jasper had sent through the appropriate channels, no doubt using his substantial influence as one of the country's richest men to see that no problems arose. Cheri saw

Jasper take a ring out of his jacket pocket and hand it to Jake.

The judge took a small book off a shelf and asked her and Jake to stand in front of him. Jasper and the two painters stood to one side. Before she could take in what was happening, she found herself repeating vows and heard Jake doing the same. She didn't look at him the whole time, nor did she sense from her peripheral vision that he looked at her, not even when he slipped the ring on her finger. The words *until death do us part* were still echoing in her ears as the judge smiled at them and proclaimed, "By the power vested in me by the State of Washington, I pronounce you man and wife."

Cheri tried to smile. She glanced at Jake for the first time since the vows started. He wore the same sort of vague smile she imagined she must have.

"You may kiss now," Judge Akins said, studying them with amusement.

Jake's expression changed and his brows drew together darkly. It was as if he'd had enough of the situation.

Cheri felt embarrassed. "Maybe later," she told the judge.

"Okay, it's your wedding," he said jauntily. "Congratulations!" After he shook hands with Jake and then Cheri, he took a couple of campaign buttons out of his pocket and gave them each one. "By the way, I'm up for re-election this year. Need your votes! Hope you'll remember me on election day!" he told them, apparently forgetting they weren't even registered to vote in his state. He glanced at his watch. "I have to leave. The wedding papers are on the bookshelf ready to be signed. You're welcome to remain here for a few minutes if you wish. Just stay out of the painters' way."

He shook hands with Jasper and then left the room.

As she slipped the campaign button into her pocket, Cheri had an unpleasant feeling in the pit of her stomach. From the look on Jake's face, she speculated that he must feel about the same as she, if not worse. She noticed him tossing his button onto the drape-covered desk.

Jasper watched them, beaming, as they signed the documents. "Well, it's done! I have a little wedding present for you," he said, walking to the niche between a bookcase and the door, where he'd left his briefcase.

"But the matching Re-elect Judge Akins buttons were so special," Jake muttered sarcastically. His eyes acquired even more malaise as he watched his father draw something out of the case. "I told you, Dad—"

"It's nothing, just a little homemade gift for you," Jasper said. "Bea wrapped it for me." He handed Cheri a package done up in crisp white tissue paper and tied with a silver bow. "I made it myself, just for you. Open it."

Cheri smiled as she took the gift, which weighed very little. Jasper seemed so happy about it, she didn't want to disappoint him. She opened the package quickly, trying to appear eager and curious. Tearing the tissue paper, she was surprised to find an old-fashioned-looking needlepoint pillow. A heart composed of multicolored flowers was stitched across it, and inside the heart in quaint lettering was written Cheri and Jake, plus today's date.

Cheri didn't know whether to cry or laugh. She felt touched that Jasper had gone to such trouble to stitch a lovely pillow just for them. On the other hand, the circumstances of their wedding were so ludicrous that to receive a tapestry pillow, something meant to be handed from generation to generation, to commemorate a marriage that was intended to be only temporary, seemed hysterically funny. And then she remembered Jake explaining to her on the phone that Jasper secretly hoped they'd fall in love and stay married. Her confused emotions merged into sadness suddenly. Poor Jasper had such high hopes for a marriage that had started like a sitcom and would probably end like a canceled TV show. She felt sorry, knowing he'd be disappointed.

She tried to smile. "Thank you, Jasper. This is very lovely. You really made this?"

"Took up needlepoint while I was recovering. I thought it turned out well, too. Hope the colors go with your furniture."

"I'm sure it will look beautiful with anything," Cheri murmured. She glanced up to catch Jake's reaction to all this. What she saw almost alarmed her.

He was staring at the innocuous-looking pillow as if it were something ominous or even dangerous. His eyes had widened so that she could see the whites of them all around his brown irises. He seemed to have grown a shade paler. She sensed he was avoiding looking at her, but he gave his father a sharp glance. "How *thoughtful*, Dad." His voice had a marked undertone that wasn't at all pleasant. Cheri wondered why he was reacting so harshly.

Jake jerked his coat lapels together and buttoned one button. "Let's get out of here. We have planes to catch." He walked toward the door, leaving them to follow.

She looked at Jasper. The older man was smiling, as if genuinely amused. He merely winked at Cheri, took her arm and led her out the door behind Jake.

Apparently she was going to get no insight as to the secret meaning behind the pillow. Rich people sure were odd.

At the Seattle airport an hour later, Jake was still fuming and had difficulty saying goodbye to his dad, who was flying back to Chicago. Cheri made up for it by giving her temporary new father-in-law a warm hug.

After Jasper's plane took off, Jake and she, cat carriers in hand, began walking to another section of the airport to meet the private plane, arranged by Jasper, that would fly them to Anacortes.

The pillow had reminded Jake of a story his brother Charles had told at his and Jenny's wedding reception, about a needlepoint pillow Jasper had made for them. The gift had sounded merely curious, maybe eccentric, to Jake, until Charles explained that Jasper had stitched their names into the pillow long before Charles and Jenny had even *thought* of marrying each other.

Charles had humorously explained that Jasper had invented "needlepoint voodoo." Apparently the old man had some idea that stitching names into a pillow sent out mysterious vibrations into the universe that made the wedding match he wanted to happen actually *happen*. At the time, Jake had laughed, but Charles, joking perhaps, had cautioned him not to underestimate Jasper's new pastime. "We did get married, much to our surprise!" he had said. "Maybe Dad's on to something." Then he had happily rushed off to dance with his bride, and Jake had dismissed the whole idea.

But now he and Cheri had received a similar pillow. Sure, they thought their marriage was only a temporary arrangement, but Jasper wanted it to be permanent, and he'd gotten out his personal new weapon to use on them. Jake began to wonder when, in fact, he'd stitched the pillow. Maybe the needlepoint voodoo had already influenced him and Cheri to agree to the marriage.

Jake's unsettling train of thought was interrupted by Cheri.

"Are you...upset about the wedding?" she asked shyly, hesitantly.

Jake felt self-conscious. He'd sort of forgotten she was there, he'd been so caught up in his own anger. "It wasn't one of my life's better experiences," he said in a dry tone, trying to show some humor.

"I know. I felt a little sick to my stomach during the ceremony," she said. "Maybe it was the paint fumes."

This made Jake laugh. "The whole scene was like something out of Laurel and Hardy. I'm surprised the ladder didn't fall and land on someone's head."

Cheri began to laugh, too. "And the judge wanting everyone to vote for him in the next election! I hope I never see him again." She was quiet for a moment. "Not that it was his fault. Maybe what made me sick was that I felt so dishonest taking the vows—'till death do us part' and all that."

Jake nodded grimly. "I know. I felt the same way." He glanced at her and saw her worried, guilt-ridden expression. She truly was a sincere person, he realized; she had a strong sense of honesty.

They came to the area where they were to catch their private plane. After inquiring, they were told to wait, that the plane would be ready to take them momentarily. After setting Dude's carrier on the floor next to Cheri's cat carrier, Jake sat down with Cheri. He took a moment to study her as she looked at the pillow, running her fingers over the letters that spelled their names. At the judge's office, he'd given her only a cursory glance, since he'd been distracted by the disarray of the office and the ceremony itself.

As he observed her now, her long hair falling forward over her buttoned jacket, he realized she was attractive, in an unsophisticated, homespun way—sort of like a corn-fed Heather Locklear without the makeup and the blond frosting. She seemed the epitome of the proverbial girl-next-door. Perhaps being a waitress, always working around food, made it hard for her to keep a trim figure. She looked a bit plump, though it was hard to tell accurately with the puffy, down-filled jacket she wore.

Most important was that she seemed pleasant and good-natured, the type who tried to make the best of a situation. This was a blessing, he realized, considering the totally abnormal situation they found themselves in, all because of Jasper's wishes—and his will. Jake reminded himself that in the end, it would all be for a good cause. His year on the island would produce a useful meteorologic study, would result in a half-million dollar donation to his Department and, someday, much more in inheritance money that he could channel into whatever scientific endeavors he thought were valuable. Even if the wedding vows were dishonest, at least they would result in something good. He wanted her to feel better about it, too.

"Don't feel guilty, Cheri. Look at it this way—this marriage will never be consummated. So it won't be a real one, and the vows we took won't count for anything. We can probably get the marriage annulled when the year is over, and it'll be as if the wedding never happened. So why not just start pretending *now* that it never did? Tell yourself it must have been a scene from some comic movie you saw and can't remember anymore."

Cheri looked up and smiled at him. She had a very pretty smile, which brightened her eyes. He noticed they were a radiant shade of aqua blue. "That sounds good," she said. "Why get hung up on the wedding when it's not a real marriage, anyway?" She nodded. "It makes sense. I'm glad you thought of that. Thanks." She glanced down again at the pillow in her hands. "Poor Jasper, though. He wants to believe it's real."

Jake exhaled in a huff. "Poor Jasper! He may have more up his sleeve than we realize. He promised to visit us on the island from time to time."

"Just for dinner," Cheri said. "I don't mind."

"It's to monitor us—see how we're doing," Jake warned her.

"Well, that's okay. We'll both be working hard."

"It's not work he's worried about."

"Oh." Cheri's expression grew concerned as she caught his drift. "He hopes we'll be working on producing another grandchild."

"They may prove to be interesting dinners," Jake said sarcastically. "He'd better not bring us any pillows with kids' names on them."

Cheri's brows drew together, as if she didn't understand. "In the judge's chambers, you looked kind of aghast when he gave us this pillow. Do needlepoint pillows have some significance in your family?"

"They didn't used to," Jake said. "They do now." He explained to her his father's mischief in his brother's life, about the presumptive wedding pillow he'd made.

"'Needlepoint voodoo'?" she said, breaking out in laughter. "That's the funniest thing I ever heard! Oh, it was just a coincidence with your brother. You can't be taking it seriously—a scientist like you?"

Her amusement suddenly made Jake see that he may have gotten carried away. He began to laugh at himself. "I'm glad you said that. I feel a little silly now." He gave her a steady look of approval. "You know, you're okay! This may work out well, after all. I bolstered your spirits a few minutes ago, and now you've returned the favor. I think we'll make good housemates."

"I do, too," she agreed. "I feel better, now that we've had this laugh."

Someone tapped Jake on the shoulder. He turned to find a man in a pilot's uniform speaking to him. "Mr. Derring? Our Lear jet to Anacortes is ready to take off. And the seaplane pilot has been notified and will be standing by to fly you from there to the island. Ready to leave?"

"You bet!" Jake said, feeling positive about this venture for the first time.

* * *

The short flight to the small airport at Anacortes was uneventful. Cheri got off the plane feeling exhilarated nevertheless. She'd never been in a private luxury plane before, and she'd spent the entire flight gazing out the window at Puget Sound and the mountain ranges surrounding it. And now she and Jake were being driven a few miles to a small harbor to meet their seaplane.

When they got out of the shuttle vehicle, another pilot came up as Jake was setting Dude's cat carrier on the ground.

"Mr. Derring? Hi, I'm Ken Pulsifer. People call me Pulse for short. I've flown your father a number of times." He extended his hand. "Glad to meet you."

Jake shook hands. "Dad said you've been flying supplies to the Millers for years."

"Yup. Nice old couple. Elsie always gives me a piece of homemade pie before I fly back."

The pilot, who looked to be somewhere around forty, had reddish hair with some gray streaks and a weathered, but handsome face. He wore a leather bomber jacket and a white scarf around his neck. Cheri's first impression was that he appeared to be a colorful local character. "Who are the Millers?" she asked.

For the first time in the conversation, both men turned to her. Immediately the pilot's eyes focused on her with interest.

"The Millers have lived on the island as caretakers of the house my dad had built there," Jake explained. "They've decided to retire and move back to the city."

"I'm flying them off the island on my way back," the pilot interjected. He extended his hand to Cheri. "I'm Pulse. And you're . . . ?"

"Cheri Weatherwax," she said, shaking his hand.

"Happy to meet you. It's nice to see a pretty face around here! Jasper Derring explained that I'm to continue bringing supplies to the island every week, so you'll be seeing me on a regular basis."

"Fine," she said, extricating her hand from his when he held on to it. "I'll do what I can to feed your pie habit," she added.

"Actually, her name is Cheri Derring now," Jake interjected rather coolly.

Cheri felt both shocked and embarrassed. Embarrassed because she'd forgotten she'd just been married, and shocked to realize that her name was legally different now.

"You're newlyweds?" Pulse asked, raising his red eyebrows at her.

"We got married a couple of hours ago, so I guess you could say we're newly wed," Cheri replied, unable to keep an odd touch of sarcasm from her voice.

The pilot nodded, still eyeing her, as if sensing there was something unusual about their situation.

"Can we leave for the island now?" Jake said with impatience.

"Sure thing!" Pulse helped carry their luggage and led them to the small seaplane tied up to a pier. After the baggage and the cat carriers were loaded in the back, they boarded the plane, which was about the size of a car with wings.

Pulse directed Cheri to sit in the front passenger seat, and Jake sat in the back. The pilot untied the plane, got in, instructed them about their seat belts and started the engines, which were rather noisy. It was raining lightly, and small water rivulets moved upward over the windshield as the plane took off over the water.

Soon they were high over Puget Sound again, heading toward a chain of islands in the distance. Before long the rain had stopped and the sun came out.

"Weather always gets better as you fly toward the islands," Pulse commented to Cheri above the sound of the engines.

"Jake's here to study the local weather," she said, just to make conversation. "He's a meteorologist."

"So you and he are going to have an idyllic long honeymoon on the island then."

Cheri grew self-conscious at the word *honeymoon* and began to feel warm with the sun shining in on her. "Guess so," she murmured.

"You guess?" The pilot grinned. "It's an ideal spot. You can go skinny-dipping on the beach. No one to see. You can do it anywhere, anytime."

By "it" Cheri didn't know if he meant skinny-dipping or sex. By his tone of voice, she was afraid he meant the latter.

"I doubt if we'll have much time for skinny-dipping, Mr. Pulsifer."

"Call me Pulse. Everyone does. Know why?"

"It's short for your last name," she said.

"Yeah. But it also reflects my personality. I'm im*pul*sive. My pulse starts racing fast under . . . certain circumstances. Part of my anatomy is always eager to *pulse*, too."

Cheri was growing very uneasy with the conversation. She turned around and looked at Jake in the backseat. He was gazing out the window, apparently at the cloud patterns, and either was not listening or could not hear them above the engines. A bit annoyed with his indifference, she faced forward again. Beginning to sweat now, she unzipped her jacket and pulled it open.

All at once she felt eyes on her, and she glanced at Pulse. He was overtly staring at her chest with an in-depth and all-inclusive gaze. Though her blouse had a high, Victorian neckline and lots of prudish lace, the silk and lace draped softly, outlining her generous curves.

Pulse studied her as if she were wearing a bikini top. She quickly pulled the jacket together again and zipped it up with an angry tug.

Her obvious displeasure did not seem to bother the pilot. He said, "You're one fine-looking woman! You get bored on that island, let me know. I can show you a good time—fly you to places you've never been while your husband's doing his meteorologic work."

"I won't have time for any excursions," she said in a firm, sharp voice. "I'll have lots of work of my own to do."

"Something wrong?" Jake asked, apparently distracted from the cloud formations by her raised voice.

Before she could answer, Pulse said in a louder voice, so Jake could hear, "Nothing's wrong. I'm just trying to chat up your bride, that's all." His tone was joking and amiable. "You've got yourself a nice gal here."

As the pilot shouted, Cheri turned around and gave Jake a telling look, trying to convey to him her displeasure.

Jake took in her facial expression, but didn't seem to know what to make of it. He lifted his shoulders and shook his head in a what-do-you-want-me-to-do manner.

Dismayed, Cheri turned and faced forward again. So much for having your new husband protect you against leering men! She tried to calm down and reminded herself that Jake apparently hadn't heard the pilot's more-than-suggestive conversation.

Fortunately, they arrived at the island less than ten minutes later. The seaplane sped up to a small pier on the shore, its pontoons skimming the water.

They got out, and Cheri could see a small, rustic wood home set in a stand of pine trees, with a flagstone walkway leading up to it. All at once the door to the house opened, and a white-haired couple came down the walk toward the pier.

Abe and Elsie Miller introduced themselves and escorted Jake and Cheri into the house. Pulse remained outside, relaxing at a picnic bench by the pier, eating a piece of pie Elsie had brought him.

After showing them around the two-bedroom house, with its large kitchen and cozy living room, Abe took Jake outside to the garden. Elsie stayed indoors with Cheri to acquaint her with the various appliances.

"The dryer seems to get overheated sometimes, so on nice days I hang my wash outside," the short, spry lady said. "There's a clothesline out back that runs from the house to a tree. As for the stove, the burners don't always light, so you have to use a match. Pulse brings us a new propane tank for the stove and heating as needed."

"He likes you," Cheri said, curious about Elsie's view of the pilot. "He told me you give him pie every time he comes."

"Oh, yes. Blueberry's his favorite," Elsie said, chuckling.

"Is he . . . reliable?" Cheri asked, fishing for more information.

"Yes, quite reliable. That's another thing you need to know. There's a grocery store and a hardware store in Anacortes that we've used for years to supply us. We call in our order on the phone, and they arrange to deliver the goods to Pulse at the dock. He flies it out to us. There's an arrangement with the post office, too, for our mail. Pulse usually comes on Mondays, but sometimes you can get him to come another day if necessary."

"What does he do?" Cheri asked. "How does he make a living?"

"He owns his own plane and hires himself out. Jasper Derring has employed him for years to take care of our needs and flies to the island with him when he visits the area. But Pulse also works for a sightseeing outfit in Anacortes. He flies tourists all around Puget Sound, over the mountains and so on."

"I see," Cheri said. She decided to change the subject. "I hear you're moving off the island permanently? I hope we aren't chasing you out."

Elsie shook her head. "No, not at all. I was relieved when Jasper called to tell us that his son and new wife were going to live on the island. He was very worried about asking us to move after we've spent almost a dozen years here. But I told him, 'Jasper, you called just when you should have.' Abe turned seventy-five last year, and we'd begun to sense it was time to move back to the city. At our age, it's not wise to live in an isolated place. You never know what health problems may arise."

"You can visit us whenever you want," Cheri said.

"Why, thank you. If we get homesick, we will. And I'll give you our new phone number when we get into our condo, so you can call if you have any questions about the house and garden here." She went to the counter, where a Crock-Pot was plugged in. "By the way, I took the liberty of putting a stew on for you and Jake for dinner. I knew you might be tired after all your plane flights, and it's hard to just start cooking in a new place. It'll be ready to eat anytime after 5:00 p.m."

"That's lovely," Cheri said, touched by her thoughtfulness. "I was wondering what I'd do about dinner."

Less than an hour later, Abe and Elsie decided they'd better leave, wanting to be in town before dark. Jake and Cheri waved goodbye to them as Pulse flew them off in the seaplane.

"They were nice, weren't they?" Cheri said.

"Extremely," Jake agreed. "We'd better see how our cats are doing. I wonder if they're still sleepy from the medications."

They went back to the house and opened both cat carriers in the living room. Dude and Cheri's cat were awake, but obviously feeling mellow and lethargic. After petting them a bit, Jake and Cheri decided to leave the animals in their carriers with the doors open, so they could come out and explore when they felt like it. Cheri found a bowl and filled it with water for them. She took a small bag of dry cat food from her luggage and poured some into another bowl.

"Good, that's the same brand I feed Dude," Jake said. "I just hope that, when they fully wake up, they don't hate each other on sight."

"We'll have to wait and see," she said, unzipping her jacket. She'd taken it off for a while when Elsie was showing her the kitchen, but she had put it back on to see the Millers off at the pier. Now she took the jacket off again and, exploring the living room, found a small closet near the door, where she hung it up. Jake had already thrown his coat on a chair, so she hung that up, too.

When she left the closet, Jake was looking over the brick fireplace, apparently trying to see if the vent was open or not.

"Going to make a fire?" she asked. "It does seem a little chilly."

"I'll get some logs from outside. Abe showed me—" Jake stopped midsentence as he turned toward her. His eyes narrowed and he appeared stunned. Cheri wondered if she'd gotten a spot on her skirt or something, but she quickly realized he wasn't looking at her skirt. He was staring at her blouse, taking in her anatomy with awe in his gaze.

"My God," he said in a hushed tone. "I didn't know you looked..."

"Looked how?" she asked with resigned patience. Somehow she hadn't expected this reaction from a highly educated man like Jake.

His reply came out as a murmured undertone. "Like a centerfold."

"Centerfold?" she repeated. "I've got on a long skirt, boots and a high-collared blouse. The only skin showing is my hands and my face."

"I can see that." His tone grew perturbed, while a hint of trepidation entered his eyes. "I didn't say you looked like you were *posing*. But you're obviously built that way... tiny waist, big... Is that really all you?"

"It's all me. I haven't had surgery." She made an attempt to laugh, but was too indignant to carry it off well. A moment ago, his reaction had seemed disappointingly typical, but his increasing displeasure confused her. "I've met lots of men, and most of them look me over, but this is the first time I've ever gotten a response like this!"

He shrugged slightly and looked askance. "Sorry. It—it just comes as a surprise, that's all. My dad never really described you to me." He cocked his head, as if an unpleasant new thought had come to him. "He probably didn't describe you *on purpose*. What a devious little plan, to talk me into a temporary marriage, and then put me on an island *alone* with... He's trying to undermine my goals, my whole life!"

Cheri impatiently ran her hand through her hair, wondering what had happened to the polite, studious stranger she'd married a few hours ago. Jake appeared so incensed right now, all because of the way she looked, that she had no idea what to say. She was used to fending men off, not having them become annoyed because she had a well-developed bustline.

"Well, we'll have to work something out," Jake said, pacing the room now.

"Work out what?" she asked.

"So we don't... run into each other a lot."

This statement made her feel doubly provoked. "There's no way we can totally avoid each other—unless you camp out on the other side of the island and cook your own food over a campfire. You're going to have to have electricity to set up your scientific equipment, aren't you? I think this house is the only source of power. Honestly, you're becoming ridiculous. This is how I look, Jake. Get used to it!''

"Get used to it? You're asking me to defy nature!"

"What's the big deal? Breast tissue is mostly fat. Think of it that way."

He slanted his eyes briefly in her direction. "Nice try, but it won't work."

"So, I guess you're a breast man, as opposed to a leg man," she quipped, trying to find some humor in the situation to deflate their flaring tempers.

Jake rubbed his forehead. "Must be," he agreed, looking very self-conscious now.

"What sort of women have you dated?" she asked, curious despite her annoyance.

"Academic types, like me. Usually with . . . trim figures," he said, as if searching for words.

"What about your female students? Some of them must be built more like me."

"I never date students," he said curtly. "It's against the rules and my personal code of ethics."

"Okay, but how do you deal with it if a voluptuous young student flirts with you? Has that ever happened?"

He seemed uneasy and shifted his weight from one leg to the other. "Yes."

"What did you do?"

"Just told myself she was off limits. I ignored her."

"Did it work?" Cheri asked. "Did she give up on you?"

"Yes."

"Okay. I'm not much older than some of your students. Think of me as one of them. And I won't even flirt with you, so it should be easy."

He made an odd sound in his throat. "But we're *living together* in the *same house.*"

"There are two bedrooms. I'll take the guest room, and you can have the main bedroom. I promise I won't walk around the house in my underwear or anything. You'll get used to the situation. You're a professor, not some teenager running on hormones."

This comment seemed to give him pause. His expression changed and he straightened his back. He grew aloof, almost remote. "You're quite right," he said in a formal manner. "Please accept my apology for my...adolescent reaction. I'll school myself to treat you with courtesy and respect."

Cheri studied him, trying to understand his change in demeanor. She was grateful for his rather stiff apology, yet it bothered her that he never looked at her once while he made it. "Don't school yourself too much or you'll become neurotic," she said. "I don't usually dress this way, anyway. I thought I should look nice for the wedding. Mostly I wear big sweatshirts and pants. If my figure is hidden, maybe you won't have such a problem with me."

Finally, he raised his eyes directly to her face, bypassing her body. "I hope so," he said with dour humor. "Otherwise it's going to be a *long* year."

5

Jake set his foot on the edge of his shovel and pressed down, sliding the blade into the rich earth. He picked up the load of soil and turned it over, then moved down the row and repeated the process. The vegetable garden would need to be planted soon, and Abe had told him it was a good idea to start turning under the remains of last year's plants early, since the job always took longer than it seemed like it ought to.

The physical exertion felt good to Jake. He'd spent the first week on the island setting up his weather station. His computer and meteorological equipment had been delivered to him piecemeal by boat and plane. He'd arranged a workstation in a corner of the living room. A satellite dish, high-tech sensors protected by an outdoor-instrument shelter, and rain gauges were all functioning properly outside the house. Jake finally had a chance to take a break from his project and do some work on the extensive garden Abe and Elsie had kept. Though it was mid-February now, the island's microclimate was delightfully sunny, with temperatures in the mid-sixties. He'd grown so warm shoveling and hoeing, he'd taken off his shirt.

Through the kitchen window, he caught a glimpse of Cheri. She was baking today, a fact he'd deduced from three clues: she'd opened the window, indicating that the kitchen had grown too warm. Once the window was open, he'd gotten wonderful whiffs of something—like maybe a cake. The remaining clue also had to do with temperature. Cheri had taken off the long sweater she'd been wearing, and now had on only a thin pink T-shirt with her jeans.

He purposely shifted his eyes to the soil, so as not to glimpse her again. God, she had curves to die for. It was damned hard to keep his mind off of her. If he was away from her for a few hours, he could submerge himself in his work. But as soon as she reappeared, near or far, his mind instantly raced to the subject he'd always before managed to sublimate and keep under control—sex. And suddenly he was the victim of his own embarrassingly adolescent lust.

That first night, when she'd told him, "You're a professor, not some teenager running on hormones," her choice of words had been uncannily apt. His personal history was a little different than that of the average American male's. Most teenage boys acted on their raging hormones, finding girls their age who were as eager to experiment as they. But Jake had always been younger than the girls in his class due to the fact that he'd skipped grades. Besides being too young, he'd been skinny, overly serious and even then had worn glasses. Girls had never looked at him twice. So, while other boys gained experience in the backseats of parked cars, Jake had never had the opportunity.

Even in college, he'd lagged behind his classmates in everything but his scholastic work. Besides being younger, he was also always the one who ruined the grading curve by getting a very high test score, a trait that did not tend to win him many friends.

Finally, in graduate school at age nineteen, he'd had his first relationship, with a college freshman he was tutoring in math. She wasn't the academic type, but she'd told him she thought he was cute, which surprised him, and he'd let himself be seduced. Their romance went on for a month or so, until her head was turned by a football player. Jake actually was not unhappy to be dumped. Though they were physically compatible, her mind was just not up to his speed. He needed women who were more cerebral and devoted to pursuing knowledge, like he was, or else he got bored with them. As the years passed and his chronological age caught up with his academic age, he found such women. Eventually there were women professors on staff with him at the university who were his age or younger. He'd dated several of them. At this point, he finally felt he'd pretty much caught up with other males in life experience.

That is, until he'd encountered Cheri. She made him realize he'd still never worked out and gotten past the adolescent lusts he'd been unable to express as a teenager. Cheri evoked that hot, helpless longing, the uncontrollable urges, the mind-numbing desire he'd felt as a frustrated teen. He was almost thirty. His hormones ought to be slowing down, not speeding up. What the hell was the matter with him?

She'd asked if he hadn't had some sexy student come on to him. Sure, he had. More than one. And yes, he'd had trouble keeping his eyes off of their curves. But he only saw them in classroom situations. They were his students, and it was easy to draw the line. They'd struck him as rather immature, anyway.

Cheri was an unsettlingly different story. She was living in the same house with him—alone on their own private island. They saw each other morning, noon and night. She was trusting and maybe naive in some ways, but she also possessed a certain maturity. She took her own life plans seriously, and for that she'd gained his respect. Yes, she was younger than he, but not too young.

And legally, she was his wife, though he tried to keep that fact out of his mind.

Jake told himself he had to keep looking upon her as if she were one of his students, exactly as Cheri had suggested. He had to admire her insight in coming up with that idea—which so far was working. Except now and then, when he caught a glimpse of her in a T-shirt, and his imagination went wild.

Stop thinking about it, he told himself as he took the shovel and hoe to the small toolshed near the house. He had scientific work to do, and he didn't need distractions. He closed up the shed and hiked to the top of a nearby ridge.

While her cake was cooling on the counter, Cheri peeked out the window toward the garden. She was disappointed to find it empty. Jake had gone off somewhere. Darn, she thought. Then she reminded herself that she shouldn't have such thoughts. About an hour earlier, she'd happened to glance out the window and found him working. He'd taken his shirt off, and she'd been surprised at how physical and masculine he looked in his jeans, with his broad chest bared. He always appeared quiet, bookish and thoughtful wearing his usual sweaters and oxford shirts. But take them off, and suddenly his whole persona changed. There was a sense of forcefulness and strength in him as he tamed the earth with his shovel. Angular shoulders, slim hips, black chest hair pointing toward his navel, muscles rippling in his arms as he worked—no scientist or professor was supposed to look that good. His glasses didn't quite fit the image, but that was okay. Cheri decided he simply looked like Superman who'd forgotten to take off his Clark Kent specs.

It was just as well he'd finished working in the garden, Cheri told herself. He might be her new husband, but she wasn't supposed to be sighing over him. Besides, with her lack of discernment, she needed to be careful about admiring *any* man. She tended to be taken in by outward appearances, only to find herself degraded by the disreputable character hidden beneath a lean, muscled body and gleaming smile.

Thank God Jake didn't smile much. He'd been so sober and aloof through their whole first week on the island that it was beginning to annoy her. She remembered the easy way they'd joked together at the airport. She'd thought they'd get along well. But then he'd had a good look at her body, and, as usually happened, it had suddenly changed everything. Except that, while most men grew more interested, Jake grew more remote.

At least she felt safe with him. He might have wound up being more like Pulse, who would probably pounce on her at every opportunity if he were living alone with her. Jake was indeed a gentleman. Maybe the first one she'd ever met.

But he was too much of one. He had an air of edgy, ivory-tower remoteness she'd never encountered before. Sometimes she had the mischievous urge to tear off her clothes and flash him, just to see what he'd do.

Of course, she wouldn't. It wasn't her style, and it was against the rules they'd agreed on. She, like he, wanted to leave the island in a year's time as free as she felt now, with no sexual baggage between them. So let him be aloof and indifferent. Why should she care?

Her brown cat jumped onto the table near the window where she was standing. She picked it up and pressed her cheek into its fur. The feline immediately began to purr. It had grown since she'd adopted it, and its fur was thick and sleek. "Hi, kitten," she cooed. "Such a good kitty. Mommy's got to think of a nice name for you." She'd thought of calling it Brownie, but that seemed too ordinary. A selection of feminine names had run through her head, like Lucy or Serena or Dixie, but somehow they didn't fit.

She walked over to the sink to look out the window at the island's low hills. It was nearing sunset, and the sky was taking on pink and salmon hues. The cat jumped out of her arms and onto the sill below the window, its green eyes riveted on something in the sky. Cheri tried to see what the cat was looking at, and when she caught sight of it, she froze.

The object appeared to be white, round and rather large as it hovered in the air, darting in one direction and then another. She wondered what it could be. No aircraft she'd ever seen looked like it or moved like it. There was no distant sound of an engine; all she heard was silence. And she was certain she wasn't mistaking it for a full moon, because it was much too large and moved far too fast.

When the object suddenly darted in the direction of the house, Cheri stopped breathing. She'd always heard of flying saucers, but had never seen one. And she knew UFOs weren't always shaped like a saucer. She'd seen people on TV talk shows who described how they'd been abducted and carried off in such spacecraft. She'd never known whether to believe their stories, but right now, staring at the strange ball in the sky, it all sounded plausible. She and Jake were alone on the island. If they were abducted, no one would even know.

"Jake!" she cried as she ran out of the house in a panic. "Jake!"

There was no response. She looked all over, ran to the front of the house and around to the other side. When she came back around the corner toward the kitchen entrance, she almost collided with a tall gray creature looming in front of her. She screamed.

"What's wrong?"

She looked up as she felt herself being grasped at the shoulders. The creature had spoken in English.

"What's the matter?" Jake asked, searching her eyes with alarm. He was wearing a gray sweatshirt with a hood drawn up over his hair.

She felt a little faint. "It's you! I thought... I was afraid..." She laughed at herself, but then remembered the object. "Jake, there's a flying saucer hovering over the island!"

"A what?"

"Flying saucer. Well, it's round and white, not like a saucer. But it was coming toward the house."

Jake began to laugh. It was nice to see him laugh, but not at this moment.

"It's true! I saw it," she insisted, fearing he wasn't going to believe her.

"It's a weather balloon," he told her. "I just went to the ridge and sent it up. It's carrying a metal box with instruments that radio back information about the temperature, humidity, air pressure and winds."

"A balloon? But it was big and darting this way and that, like UFOs are supposed to do."

"A weather balloon *is* big. The winds buffet it around as it goes up through the atmosphere. Here, I'll show you."

He led her to the back of the house and pointed up in the sky. The balloon was now much smaller than when she'd seen it before.

"There it goes," he said. "It drifts about ten miles upward into the troposphere. Pretty soon it'll be too small to see at all." He pulled the hood back off his hair. "I need to check my equipment to see that the feedback is coming in properly." He looked at her. "Are you okay now? I guess I should have warned you. I'll be sending up weather balloons twice a day, every day. It's part of my study of the microclimate."

"I'm okay," she said, a little giddy now. "Why are you wearing a gray hood? I thought you were an alien coming toward me."

"It's getting cool, and it's very windy up on the ridge, so I put the hood up," he explained. He glanced downward, noting what she was wearing. "You must be cold in that."

She'd run outside in her T-shirt, without even thinking of grabbing her sweater. His eyes took on an absorbed aspect, a subtle glow of desire building in them as he studied her figure. It was a look she'd seen many times on many men, and she regarded it as a typical male reaction. But for Jake, it was decidedly untypical, and she found herself rather enjoying it.

The moment vanished, however, when all at once, as if coming to his senses, he tore his eyes away. "Put on some warmer clothes so you don't catch cold," he instructed before turning on his heel and walking away. He went ahead of her into the house, to the corner of the living room where he'd set up his workstation.

Cheri bridled at his directive manner, but said nothing. She put on her long pink sweater and went back to work in the kitchen, frosting the cake she'd made. In about an hour, she called him for dinner. He came in wearing a new set of clothes—an oxford shirt, tweed pants and a burgundy pullover. She'd heard the shower running and guessed he needed to wash off dirt from the garden.

He took a seat at the kitchen table as she set out a roast chicken she'd made. After the side dishes were placed, she sat down herself. Her brown cat promptly jumped up on the table.

"No, no, kitty," she said, picking it up and cuddling it. "You shouldn't be up here."

"She's going to learn a lot from that tone of voice," Jake said with disapproval, opening his napkin onto his lap.

"What do you mean?"

"'No, no, kitty,'" he said, imitating her. "Your koochy-koo method sounds like you're encouraging her. She'll think 'no' means 'go right ahead, be my guest.'"

Cheri put the cat on the floor. "I don't believe in yelling at animals or swatting them with newspapers."

"You don't have to do that. But you need to sound firm with them. You'll never catch Dude jumping up on the table."

She glanced at Jake wryly. "No, because Dude is too fat to jump up on anything. And if you're going to teach me about discipline, what method have you been using to put him on a diet?"

Jake exhaled and stroked his nose. "Okay, you win that round."

"I'm not trying to have a verbal boxing match with you," she said.

"Men and women just can't avoid the battle of the sexes, can they?"

She drew her eyebrows together. "Battle of the sexes? We're talking about cats, aren't we?"

"Right," he quickly agreed, seeming anxious to change the subject. "Are you going to carve this chicken, or do I just rip off a leg?"

Boy, is he in a mood, she thought to herself as she began to cut up the chicken with a serrated knife. She served him a drumstick and thigh, and then served herself.

He took off his glasses and set them on the table before picking up his knife and fork, as he did at every meal. So far she hadn't felt comfortable enough to ask why. But at the moment, she was feeling persnickety.

"How come you always take off your glasses when you eat? The stuff I cook doesn't look appetizing to you?"

He glanced up from his plate in surprise. "No, the food's been great. I'm afraid I'm going to be shaped like Dude when I get off this island."

She smiled. "I won't let that happen. You look too good to go to fat. I'll start cooking low-fat dishes, if necessary."

He was staring at her with a curious expression in his suddenly *un*moody dark eyes. But when he spoke he sounded normal—a little too normal. "I take off my glasses when I eat because I'm nearsighted. I can see the plate perfectly well without them, and glasses just seem to be in the way." He made a little chopping motion with his hand for emphasis.

Gosh, he's really adorable, Cheri realized. But then she reprimanded herself. She'd thought her former fiancé was a charmer, too. Of course, Jake was a professor and a scientist, not an out-of-work embezzler. He also was a millionaire's son and certainly not in need of her bled-dry bank account. And he was making a huge point of not wanting anything else from her, either. It was ironic—she may have finally found the perfect man. But what was she supposed to do with him? She felt strangely boxed in by invisible barriers.

"How far can you see without them?" she asked. "Can you see me clearly across the table?"

He gazed at her, an arch look creeping into his eyes. "Yes, it's a small-enough table. So don't try to get away with anything, thinking I can't see."

"What would I try to get away with?" she teased.

"I hesitate to even contemplate that. You have a mischievous side to you."

She was enjoying his banter. "I do? How?"

"You take me off guard sometimes. That comment about Dude, for example."

She smiled. "What else?"

"How's your correspondence course coming? You said you got the first installment." He shoveled peas into his mouth, as if unaware that he'd abruptly changed the subject again.

"I read through the first chapter and started the workbook assignments. I'm afraid Basic Accounting may not be all that basic for me. I peeked ahead, and it looks pretty tough."

"Just take it a chapter at a time. Don't scare yourself by jumping ahead."

"Are you good at mathematical things?" she asked.

"I've always been good at math."

"If I run into problems, would you help explain them to me? I may need a private tutor," she said with a rueful chuckle.

He almost choked on his food. When he'd swallowed and composed himself, he said in his most professorial tone, "Only if absolutely necessary. You really should learn it on your own. You won't always have me around to explain things to you."

"Okay," she said, embarrassed at having asked him for a favor. "Sorry."

He said nothing and continued eating. The tension at the table was thick enough to slice, though she didn't know why. After a few long moments of uncomfortable silence, Cheri said in a light tone, "I'm still trying to think up a name for my kitty. Any ideas?"

His stiff demeanor relaxed a bit. He lifted his shoulders. "How about Truffles?"

"That's good," she said. "Because she's brown like a chocolate truffle." She brought her fingertips to her mouth as a new idea came to her. "I know—how about Tiramisu? I can call her Tira for short."

"What's that? Japanese?"

"Italian," she said. "Tiramisu is an Italian dessert. It's made with ladyfingers dipped in espresso and covered with a sweet cream-cheese mixture. The top is sprinkled with powdered chocolate. Haven't you ever had it?"

"No."

"I'll make it for you sometime," she said. "If I can get the mascarpone cheese shipped in."

Jake smiled a little and pushed his empty plate away. "Sounds great. Speaking of dessert..." he said, as if hoping she'd fill in the blank.

She got up. "Sure, I have a special one tonight." She cleared away their dishes.

"I got a whiff of something good when I was digging in the garden," he said as she took the plates to the sink. "The chicken was excellent, by the way. I like the way you seasoned it. Nice and tender, too."

His comfortable expression changed when she set the cake on the table in front of him. It was heart shaped and covered with pink, butter-cream frosting.

Jake scrutinized it with increasing alarm. "What's this supposed to be?"

"It's Valentine's Day," she said with a grin. "So I made a Valentine cake."

"Valentine's Day!"

"Didn't you check the calendar? Or hear it on the radio? It's February 14."

Jake pinched the bridge of his nose. "No, I missed that bit of news. February 14 is just another day to me. Why are *we* celebrating Valentine's Day? Is this supposed to be some sort of message?"

"Message?"

"Were you expecting hearts and flowers? Just because we're married doesn't mean we're supposed to be romantic. This relationship is going to stay platonic—"

"Jake, it's just a cake. If it was Christmas, I'd bake a Christmas-tree cake. I'm practicing, that's all. When I have my own café, I'll want to observe holidays with special cakes and things."

He hesitated. "So this isn't . . . You're not . . ."

"No!" she said, indignant. "Why are you so uptight all the time? You accuse me of coming on to you because I make a cake in the shape of a heart? Give me a break!"

"I didn't know it was Valentine's Day, and it seemed . . . unusual," he said, still miffed.

"Did I spell out our names in icing?" she asked. "Did I put an arrow across it? Did I write Be My Valentine? No, I just put pink frosting on it and some sprinkles. Imagine to yourself that it's round and maybe you'll be able to choke it down."

"Okay, okay. Cut me a piece," he said in a testy voice.

As she sliced into it, she thought of the time she'd spent cutting the originally round layers into perfectly shaped hearts, which she'd piled on top of one another with a special raspberry filling in between. All that care and work, only to be accused, apparently, of trying to make a pass at him. Why would he even think such a thing?

As she set a piece of the cake on a small plate in front of him, she decided to ask. "Why would you think I'd try to send you a romantic 'message'?"

He shook his head. "I—I . . . wouldn't know."

"Have I shown any indication of throwing myself at you?"

"You asked me to tutor you," he said.

"Well, that's just . . . tutoring. There's nothing romantic about math."

"No?" he said with impatience. "I once tutored a girl in math, and the next thing I knew I was in bed with her."

Cheri stared at him, astonished. His sudden revelation reverberated in her mind. "Really?"

He shifted in his seat. "Yes, really."

"So what happened?"

"I told you, I slept with her."

"I mean after that?"

"It was just a—a... It didn't last long. It was just . . . one of those things."

"A trip to the moon on butterfly wings?" she said, teasing him with partly remembered words to an old song.

She knew she'd gone too far, for now he looked deeply annoyed. "You're speaking of my private history, so let's drop it. I haven't asked you about your past affairs."

"I haven't had any," she said matter-of-factly.

He gave her a skeptical look. "No? What about your fiancé? Something must have happened before he ran off with your money."

"No," she said. "I told him I wanted to wait till the wedding night, and he agreed. That's why I trusted him," she added with a sigh.

"So . . . you're saying you've never . . . ? You can't be a virgin!"

She felt herself blush, but was too angry to let the question embarrass her. "Why not? Because any girl built like me must have started having sex when she was thirteen? That's what *all* you guys think! In high school, the boys even wrote things like that and worse about me on the bathroom walls. Gossip flew, and pretty soon everybody believed it. My mother had to mount a single-handed campaign just to get the school to remove the graffiti and reprimand the boys. That's when I started wearing loose clothes to cover myself up. That's when my grades fell, because my self-esteem hit rock bottom. That's why I never made it to college. *And* . . . that's why I'm a virgin. Ever since high school I've hated males who looked at me that way and drew filthy conclusions. Why would I have slept with any of them? And now even you, the high-minded professor, thinks exactly the same thing." She blinked back hot tears. "So don't worry! You can relax. I'll never have any interest in sleeping with *you*, either!"

She got up from the table and walked into the living room, leaving him sitting in front of the cake. After a while, he came to the doorway.

"I'm sorry," he said to her as she sat on the couch. "I didn't mean to offend you. I shouldn't have jumped to conclusions about the cake. I'm just...edgy, for some reason. I've never lived with a woman before. You'll have to expect me to make a few mistakes. Or maybe more than a few," he said with self-deprecating humor. "And I'm sorry about your high-school experience. Men do tend to think of physically beautiful women as sex objects. We believe what we want to. We're stuck with all that testosterone, you know."

She nodded. "I know."

"Why is sex so confusing?" he asked, sounding very philosophical, yet sincere.

She shook her head wistfully. "I don't know," she said, staring at her hands in her lap.

There was a long silence. When she looked up, she found him still standing near the doorway, staring at her with a strange, faraway glow in his eyes. Her gaze seemed to alert him, and he suddenly looked self-conscious.

"You relax," he said. "I'll do the dishes."

"You don't have to," she objected.

"No, I want to. Watch some TV. You've had a long day."

She did feel a little weary just now. "Okay. Thanks. And...I'm sorry about my harangue against men. I've tried to get past that attitude. Sometimes it just comes back, though."

"We all have to get past our past," he said. He started to leave, then paused. "Where's the dish soap?"

She smiled. "Under the sink."

As Jake was drying the dishes in the kitchen, he looked out the window. The moon was full. Maybe that was the reason he was on edge—the opposing gravitational pull on the earth between the sun and the moon was always greatest at this time, giving everyone on the planet extra tension.

Dude ambled into the kitchen, having finally roused himself from his long catnap on Jake's bed. He yawned and stretched and walked over to the bowl of cat food Cheri had put in a corner of the kitchen. Tira, who had been sleeping on the cleared kitchen table, promptly jumped down and sniffed Dude's fluffy black tail. Dude turned and spat, and the smaller cat fearlessly spat back. Then she walked off into Cheri's room. Jake smiled at the little scene. The two cats had been together a week and they still hated each other.

As Dude began to chow down at the food bowl, Jake was reminded of Cheri's jibe. She was easygoing and considerate, but he'd noticed she could invent sassy comebacks with the speed of lightning when she wanted to. And she didn't hesitate to use them, either. Treating her as one of his students wouldn't work in the long run.

How should he handle the situation? Jake sighed as he put away a dish in the upper cabinet next to the sink. He didn't have a clue. The image of her in her T-shirt, running toward him, calling his name in fright, came to his mind. She was deliriously beautiful—long hair flying, blue eyes wide and startled, her breasts softly bouncing. When he'd grabbed her by the shoulders to calm her down, she'd felt warm and incredibly feminine. When he'd explained to her about sending up the weather balloon, the changing expressions on her face as she realized she'd mistaken it for a UFO were adorable. She was so genuine and guileless. It was his own wayward thoughts that made him ready to assume she was trying to send a message with that cake.

She was a virgin, too. He felt terribly experienced by comparison, and also protective of her. She really was a rare find. He had to give his father credit. It was every man's fantasy to be stuck alone on an island with a curvacious, twenty-three-year-old virgin. And his resourceful dad had managed to create exactly that situation just for him. He ought to be touched. *The conniving old manipulator,* Jake thought. *If he believes he can undermine me—*

His inner tirade was interrupted by the phone ringing. "I'll get it, Cheri," he yelled, as he walked to the corner of the kitchen counter where the phone was. "Hello?"

"Hi, Jake. It's Dad. Just calling to see how the newlyweds are doing."

Sometimes Jake could swear his father had ESP. "That's funny, I was just thinking about you. How are you and Mom?"

"Very well, thank you. We just had a nice Valentine's Day dinner out. How about you and Cheri?"

"Um, yeah, she baked a heart-shaped cake," Jake responded dutifully, wondering why people got so hyped-up about Valentine's Day.

"How lovely." Jasper sounded truly pleased. "Isn't she the dearest girl?"

"She ... great, Dad."

"That's all? Just 'great'?"

"Easy to get along with, too," Jake added, knowing he was being prodded. What did his dad expect? That Jake would admit he couldn't keep his mind off of her, that just watching her breathe was a major distraction, that sometimes he wondered how he'd get through the day without pulling her into his arms?

"And?" Jasper still seemed to be fishing for more.

"Look, Dad," Jake said, lowering his voice so Cheri couldn't overhear him in the living room, "I know what you want to happen, why you arranged this whole marriage, but it's not *going* to happen. She's made it clear she doesn't want to have a relationship with me, and I've made it clear that I don't want one, either. So we're agreed. We get along just fine as we are—as *friends*."

"You seem to be talking about it, though," Jasper said.

"About what?"

"Sex?" Jasper innocently suggested.

"Yes! We've agreed..." Jake stopped before going further. He tried to keep his temper under control. "Dad, what right do you have to try to manipulate my sex life?"

"You never seemed to have one, so I just thought I'd make it easier for you."

Jake would have liked to slam the phone down, but he didn't. The fact was he'd managed to keep the relationships he had with women quiet. Because he lived in Wisconsin, his parents never met his girlfriends. He liked it that way, always sensing how curious his father was about his personal life.

Jake was different than his brothers, who had grown up normally, without skipping grades. They were forever bringing girls around. They also were more like Jasper, aggressive and entrepreneurial. Jasper had always wanted his youngest son to be more like his older brothers.

When he'd regained control of his anger, Jake said carefully, "Dad, I'm old enough to figure out what I want for myself, and I don't need any help from you."

"Okay, all right," Jasper said with equanimity. "Speaking of you being old enough, your thirtieth birthday is about six weeks from now. I have some business to take care of in San Francisco then. I thought I'd fly up to see you for the day—help you celebrate."

Jake rolled his eyes. He'd just as soon people would forget his birthday. "Sure, that's fine. Is Mom coming, too?"

"I'll see what I can do. She doesn't like to fly, you know."

"It is pretty complicated getting here. She probably wouldn't like the seaplane at all," Jake agreed. His mother tended to have problems with motion sickness on plane flights.

"I'll try, though," Jasper said. "Can I say hello to Cheri?"

The request took Jake a bit by surprise. "Sure." As he put down the phone to get Cheri, he realized he'd forgotten that his parents and she had formed their own little relationship. It made Jake uneasy. He knew how to keep his father in hand, but Cheri might not.

He went to the living room to get Cheri. She smiled brightly and hurried into the kitchen. Jake sat down on the couch and rubbed his face with his hands, feeling tense and out of sorts again.

He heard Cheri's voice coming from the kitchen. He couldn't make out everything she said, but she seemed to be lighthearted and joking. He liked the way she laughed. It almost made him jealous that his father brought out her insouciant nature so easily.

Jake was sitting on the couch glumly when she ended the brief phone conversation and came back into the living room.

"He's coming for your birthday," she said with excitement.

"I can't wait," Jake said.

"You're not looking forward to turning thirty?" she asked, sitting on an upholstered chair near him. The infamous needlepoint pillow was there, and she moved it to one side.

"My age doesn't bother me, but my dad does. You realize he's coming to check on us," Jake told her with asperity. He pointed toward the pillow next to her. "He wants to see if his voodoo has taken hold."

"Oh, it'll be fun. We'll just tease him back."

Jake shook his head. "I wish it were that simple."

"He means well," Cheri said.

Her face was so sweet, even angelic, just now that Jake had to look away. He didn't know how to behave around her anymore. In his mind, the situation was getting worse by the minute. His dad would only add to the confusion.

A few weeks went by. Jake managed to get his meteorologic study fully underway, analyzing the data his instruments were gathering. Cheri continued to impress him with her cooking skills. Jake was afraid he'd be tempted to keep her around when their year was up just to continue eating so well. But he faced worse temptations where she was concerned, and he constantly feared he'd forget his resolve not to touch her.

Another irritation confronted him once a week. Whenever Pulse flew in, bringing their supplies, Jake would help him carry the goods into the house. He couldn't avoid noticing that the pilot's eyes were invariably fixed on Cheri's anatomy, no matter how covered up she was. It annoyed him that Cheri seemed to feel duty bound to give the flying Don Juan a slice of her latest dessert. Pulse would sit in the kitchen leisurely eating it with the cup of coffee she'd serve him. Jake always felt he needed to stick around the whole time the pilot was on the island to make sure he didn't get out of line with Cheri. The guy had a lot of gall to stare that way at another man's wife!

But other than that weekly disruption, Jake and Cheri had fallen into a comfortable routine, each working separately through the day and eating together in the evening. He usually got up earlier than she and made his own breakfast. Abe had told him that there was a path that went around the entire island. Jake found the head of the trail about fifty yards from the pier and began jogging part of the way up and back each morning for exercise. By the time he returned, Cheri was usually up and dressed, which saved them from any accidental semiclothed encounters. At lunch, she usually brought him a sandwich, which he ate at his computer or wherever he was working.

Today, he'd finished his sandwich a couple of hours ago and was bringing his plate back into the kitchen on his way to do some gardening. He found Cheri in jeans, a large sweatshirt and athletic shoes, tying back her hair with a clip.

"Going somewhere?" he asked.

"I'm getting cabin fever, so I decided to see if I can walk all the way around the island," she said. Like Jake, she would often hike on the trail for exercise. She didn't have a daily routine, however. "I've been about halfway, I think. Pulse said there's a beach somewhere, so I thought I'd look for it. The island's about eight miles around, isn't it? I should be able to get back before dark, right?"

Jake felt a little uneasy about letting her go alone to a part of the island he hadn't seen himself yet. He wondered if the terrain got rough. "That sounds about right. But if the trail gets difficult, then maybe you'd better come back the way you came. You don't want to sprain an ankle and be stuck out there."

She smiled quietly, as if touched by his concern. "I'll be okay. I'm not a helpless little kid."

She seemed to think he was worrying about her. He didn't want her to draw that conclusion. "You're right. You'll be fine. I won't give it another thought."

Her expression changed and she gave him a nod. "See you later."

As she walked out, he wanted to say, "Be careful," but he restrained himself from doing so. If *he* wasn't careful, he was going to get emotionally attached to her. He had to look upon her only as a temporary friend, because in ten months they'd be saying goodbye.

As he went toward the toolshed, he looked at the western sky, noting the clouds. The rest of the sky was sunny, but there was a dark, heavy formation on the southwestern horizon, over the Olympic Mountains. He knew there was a big storm coming in over the Pacific, and he wondered if the mountains would do their usual magic and keep the rains away from the island. He was afraid this storm might just beat the odds.

Instead of opening the toolshed, he turned and went back into the house. He brought up the Doppler radar map on his computer screen and could see exactly where rain was already falling. He noted the increasing wind speed and direction, the falling barometer and the changing temperature. This was one of those times when meteorologists wished they were soothsayers who could predict the future. Jake guessed it was a fifty-fifty chance they'd get rain in the next hour or so. He might as well toss a coin. The very purpose of his yearlong study was to learn how the microclimate worked more precisely, so that someday such a prediction could be far more accurate.

He checked the National Weather Service to see what they were saying. Their estimate was fifty-fifty, the same as his. Damn, he thought. He went back outside and climbed the ridge to get a better look. When he reached the high point, his instincts told him the darkening skies would not bypass the island. He'd better go after Cheri and tell her to come back, or she might get soaked.

Jake headed down the trail at a fast speed. Cheri must have been walking at a quick pace, too, because it took him over twenty minutes to catch up with her.

"Cheri," he called, coming up behind her.

She turned in surprise. "Jake! You decided to walk around the island, too?"

"No. I came to warn you. There's a big storm coming in. We may get doused in a little while. I think we should go back. You can walk the island another day."

She blinked and then smiled. Lifting her hand toward the clear, sunny sky, arching blue over the sound and the other islands in the distance, she said, "How's it going to rain?"

"Turn around and look southwest," he said.

She did. "Oh. But it usually doesn't hit us. Remember you said that the mountains keep the islands dry—"

"It doesn't always work that way. This storm's a biggie. So let's go."

She held her ground and looked at the southwestern sky again. "Nah, I don't think it'll rain."

"Cheri, I saw the storm on radar. I know more about weather than you."

She made a face, twisting her adorable mouth to one side. "Oh, okay, Mr. Weatherman. You'd better be right. If it doesn't rain, you won't get dessert tonight."

Jake laughed. "I'll chance it."

"It's tiramisu. Made it fresh this morning. Better think about it."

"Let's go!" he said firmly, taking her by the arm to pull her along.

"Oh, now we're using caveman tactics to get the little woman to do what we want?"

Jake promptly let go of her arm. "Just keep up with me, okay?"

"Yes, sir."

He hurried her down the trail. In ten minutes, the sky had darkened considerably. The air temperature felt as if it had fallen by several degrees. In twenty minutes, the atmosphere was ominous. Low, black, cumulonimbus clouds scudded over the trees. He was glad when they reached the clearing near the pier and the house was in sight.

It was at that moment, however, when the clouds opened up and they were caught in a chilling downpour.

Cheri drew the back of her sweatshirt up over her head. "We're going to get drenched!" she exclaimed, beginning to run.

He ran along beside her, his arm protectively around her. "We would have made it to the house if you hadn't wasted time arguing with me."

"Okay, you were right. You can have two pieces of dessert," she said as they reached the door.

They walked into the kitchen, their clothes so saturated they left trails of water on the linoleum floor.

"God, it's freezing," Cheri said through chattering teeth.

Jake quickly shed his dripping jacket. "Take off your wet clothes." He proceeded to take off his own sweater and shirt.

When she pulled the heavy wet sweatshirt over her head, he saw she was wearing a jogging top, the tight, form-fitting kind women wore to work out. As she stood there shivering, her hair wet, her arms crossed under her breasts, he thought she was the most exquisite thing he'd ever seen. He hadn't realized until now how slim she actually was. What made her so truly beautiful, though, was the way she was looking at him. She was staring at him and his bared chest like a soft-eyed waif longing for warmth and comfort. There was a yearning in her glistening eyes....

Before he realized it, he was taking her in his arms, wanting to warm her body with his, wanting to hold her. She yielded to his embrace readily, yet as if not quite knowing what was happening. Pressing herself to him, she wound her arms around his back, hugging him. Her firm breasts jutted into his chest, instantly arousing him, making him want her. Just a kiss, he told himself. For just one kiss, he could live through this fierce desire, and die happy.

As if sensing his need, she turned her face to him. In an instant their lips met. The soft heat of her mouth against his radiated through him and seemed to melt his bones. A whimpering sound came from her throat and she sank into him, all the while clinging to his lips as if she didn't want to ever let go. An overwhelming sense of strength and power came over Jake. He had the feeling, the devastating insight, that he could do anything and she wouldn't object.

His breathing grew heavy as he continued the kiss. He slid his hand upward to the side of her breast to caress what he had coveted for weeks. Flattened slightly against his chest, her rounded breast felt firm and plump in his palm. She turned a bit, as if purposely enabling him to cradle her entire breast in his hand. His thumb found the peak of her nipple through the damp cloth. She moaned softly with pleasure and moved her fingers up into his hair. His desire escalating higher and higher, he slid his mouth to her chin and down her neck, kissing her hotly. She seemed to quiver with each kiss, tilting her head back invitingly. He kissed her collarbone and then hovered over the voluptuous cleavage harnassed by her jogging top. His mouth burned into her soft mounds of flesh while his hand caressed her more and more aggressively.

"Oh, Jake," she half whispered, half moaned. He was barely aware at first that her hand had gone to her shoulder. She began sliding the thick strap down her arm. All he knew was that there was more silken skin for his mouth to cover with sliding kisses. And then his mouth fastened hungrily on her pink, pert nipple. As he suckled her she gave a little scream of joy.

Somehow the sound brought him to his senses. He lifted his head and looked at her. Her green-blue eyes were glazed with desire and half-closed with pleasure

"Don't stop," she said with an eager, almost drunken smile. She pushed his hand upward to cover her nipple. "I want this, Jake." She stretched to kiss him on the mouth. He backed his head away. When she looked startled, he let her go.

"Jake—"

"You're an amazingly wanton virgin!" he blurted out, breathing raggedly, his head spinning. "Are you trying to seduce me?"

Her expression changed and then her whole demeanor grew self-conscious. Her smile disappeared and she pulled the strap back onto her shoulder, covering herself up. "You kissed me," she said, looking confused.

"Okay, we kissed," he admitted, unsure how it had come about. "But now you seem willing to do a lot more than kiss."

"I thought . . . you wanted . . ."

"Yeah, I lost my head for a minute there." He backed away a step, still breathless. "But what did we agree on before we ever got to this island?"

She bowed her head. "That—that we'd keep it platonic."

"Right. Is kissing me and baring your—yourself keeping things platonic?" He raked his hand through his wet hair.

"No."

"Why were you pulling down your top then?"

She looked at him, her face a little stunned. "Because you were kissing me there, and I thought you wanted more."

He blinked, knowing she was right. But he needed to be firm with her, if he could, or they might *really* go astray. "You were the one saying 'Don't stop. I want this.' How can we keep ourselves in line if you behave this way? I'm only human. I'll respond! We'll wind up in a relationship, and then where will we be? All our plans out the window!''

She lifted her chin in an indignant manner. ''You kissed me. You started it. If you want things to stay platonic, then don't move toward me with heat sizzling in your eyes. Don't start kissing me and touching me. I'm human, too. I only kissed back because you seemed to be enjoying it.'' She glared at him in anger. ''You men never shoulder your share of the blame for anything!'' She turned abruptly, ran into her bedroom and closed the door. He heard her lock it.

Alone now, Jake took a deep breath, wondering how all this had happened. He noticed his hands were shaking. He was still uncomfortably hard beneath his zipper, too. God, it made him dizzy how fast she could turn him on. It amazed him that she was so innocent, yet she had acted with such abandon with him. He was positive she would have been willing—no, eager—to go to bed with him!

The thought weakened his knees, and he sat down on a chair by the kitchen table. He wiped moisture off his forehead with the heel of his hand. Well, one thing was clear. *His* resolve to keep their relationship platonic was a lot stronger than *hers*. Her willpower was about as resilient as custard. It was going to be up to *him*, it seemed, to keep them on the straight and narrow. She was too naive to even understand her own desire for him—and how dangerous it could be.

In her room, Cheri sank onto the bed in tears and confusion. She was certain that he'd wanted her as much as she'd wanted him. She'd felt his seeking hands, his hot breath on her skin, the heaving of his chest against her breasts from his labored breathing. Cheri had been in enough sticky situations to know when men were in the heat of desire and ready for sex. Usually she found it very distasteful. This was the first time she'd ever responded, the first time it had ever felt good and right to her. She'd grown to trust Jake. He seemed to see her as a person, not as some well-endowed "babe." But then when she gave in, actually enjoying a man's caresses for the first time, he'd turned on her. He still had the same mind-set as when she'd baked him that cake, only worse. Now he'd accused her of trying to seduce him!

Well, she had to admit, she would have been willing.... She found him more and more attractive. And being a virginal twenty-three-year-old, she was curious about sex. Jake seemed safe. He had some integrity. Maybe half consciously, half unconsciously, she'd been thinking that he might be the ideal man to allow to arouse her, to explore lovemaking with.

She wiped away a tear and felt guilty. Maybe it *was* her fault. It had all happened so suddenly. They'd come in from the rain, soaked. She'd been shivering, and he'd said, very logically, that they should take off their wet clothes. And then she'd seen his gorgeous chest...and the next thing she knew, they were kissing.

But even as she relived those moments now, it still seemed to her that *he* had moved first. She was standing there looking at him, and *he'd* taken a step toward her. And then she was in his arms. And the kiss...the kiss was mutual. It had just...happened. How could he accuse her of trying to seduce him?

She did start to pull down her top, though, she reminded herself, trying to be fair. But even then, she'd done it in response to him. He was kissing her so aggressively, she knew he wanted more. And she'd felt very willing to give him more. But did that make it all *her* fault?

No! she decided. How dare he accuse her of being a seductress? He was no better than any other male on the planet, damn him! She'd thought he was different. She'd thought finally, *finally*, she might have met a man she could trust and respect. But they always turned on you, one way or another.

New tears slid from her eyes. The trouble was, it was a little too late to just cross Jake off. She still found him extremely attractive, even though he was being unfair to her. Must be her gullible nature getting the better of her again! She'd begun to want him, a little more every day. Her desire had crept up on her unexpectedly. Now she longed to lose her virginity with him. And he wouldn't let her have him. He was too set on honoring their agreement, of not letting a relationship muddy the waters during their year on the island. But it seemed to Cheri that their torrid kiss had already muddied up things between them. She didn't see that their stupid pact meant much in the face of the overpowering physical pull between them.

So the hell with Jake! she decided. From now on she'd act as *she* wished and dress as *she* wished, with no more deference to his wishes or his vulnerabilities. If he was going to make her out to be Eve with the apple, then he might as well play the role of Adam here in their little Garden of Eden. It was totally up to Jake to see if he had any more willpower than the first father of all *man*kind!

6

One morning a few weeks later, Cheri put on a new outfit she'd ordered from a catalog. She'd found the catalog featuring clothing for women of all ages in the mail. Pulse had delivered it the day after the event Cheri had privately dubbed The Kiss. The catalog had been addressed to Elsie Miller or Current Resident. Cheri had some money left from her last paycheck at Tucci's, and she decided to order some things from the catalog before forwarding it to Elsie. The clothes she chose weren't fancy or expensive, but they were youthful, colorful and definitely not oversize—items like scoop-necked knit tops, tank tops and shorts. Warmer weather was coming, she rationalized. Why should she have to sweat in bulky clothes?

She elected to wear a short-sleeved knit top with blue-and-white horizontal stripes, and some tight-waisted, lightweight, blue denim overalls with a bib and thick straps that crossed in the back. Putting them on and looking at herself in the mirror on the inside of her bedroom door was a treat—she'd rarely worn anything stylish or kicky in several years.

After combing her hair, she walked into the kitchen to have some cereal for breakfast. While she was washing her dishes after eating, Jake walked in from his morning jog. He mumbled, "Hello," and she mumbled the same back to him. Their demeanor toward one another since The Kiss had been studiously indifferent, though still polite. He'd adopted this sort of manner with her, and Cheri had followed suit, for the time being.

Jake barely looked at her, but he stopped in the middle of the kitchen and said, "How come you're up early today, too?"

"Tira woke me. She was meowing a lot. I was afraid something was wrong, but she seems okay."

"That's right—she was meowing in the middle of the night," Jake said, as if remembering. "Woke me up. Made Dude kind of agitated—he jumped off my bed and started clawing on the door." He paused as he took in the clothing she was wearing. "Where'd you get an outfit like that?"

"A catalog," she said coolly. "Like it?"

"It's a little showy."

"Is it?"

"Yes."

"So?"

"So why are you wearing it?" he asked, sounding impatient. "Why did you buy it? You like to be more covered up than that."

"I do?"

"Yes!"

"No," she contradicted. "I never *liked* dressing sloppy. I did it so men wouldn't think I was trying to be 'showy.' This outfit is ordinary, Jake. You must have seen lots and lots of young women wearing clothes like this every day on campus."

He studied her suspiciously. "You're up to more mischief, aren't you?"

This took Cheri aback. "Mischief? Because I put on a new outfit?"

"I think maybe you've hatched a plan. You've decided to start dressing provocatively to try to lure me into a relationship."

She placed her hands on her hips, ready to take him on. "First of all, this is not a provocative outfit. There's no short skirt, no cleavage showing, nothing—"

"It outlines your figure pretty darn well!" he interrupted.

"So what? Lots of women's clothes, even ladies' business suits, show off a woman's figure. What I'm wearing is not out of the ordinary! If you see it as provocative, then that's *your* problem, Jake. That's for *you* to deal with by yourself, on your own. I've dressed in big clothes for years, trying to keep men from thinking the wrong things about me. No more. From now on, I'm dressing to please myself!"

She let that sink in for a moment. He stood there looking thoroughly annoyed, but he didn't seem to have any response.

"As for luring you—sorry, you can give up that fantasy! You've proven again that you're just like all the rest, so why would I want you?" She tried to put more conviction into her tone than she actually felt. Even as he stood there glowering at her, she longed to startle him by ripping off his glasses and covering his stern mouth with an impulsive kiss.

"I'm not buying this, Cheri," he said.

She wet her lips with her tongue. Had he seen through her, read desire in her eyes, though she was protesting having any? "What do you mean?" she challenged.

"I think you've decided you'd like this temporary marriage to become permanent. That's why you're ordering sexy clothes. You figure that if you can entice me into bed, then you'll have me in the palm of your hand. Maybe you've decided being married to a millionaire's son isn't such a bad deal. You'd have all the money you ever want for the rest of your life—and you wouldn't have to open any café, either.''

Suddenly her confused feelings about Jake resolved into outrage. "How dare you make me out to be a gold digger!''

''You're claiming you aren't one? You agreed to this 'marriage' because my father offered you a million dollars. That's a pretty big clue right there. In fact, that's a major piece of evidence!''

Cheri's temper flew into high gear. "I told Jasper I didn't want a million. I asked him to replace what was stolen from me, so I could set myself up in business—so I wouldn't have to be married at all. I don't want to be legally hitched to you or any other man! That was never, ever, in any way, shape or form, my *goal.*''

''Of course,'' he said sarcastically, his jaw taut. He walked out of the room. She heard his bedroom door slam. Soon she heard the shower running.

Realizing a tear was streaming down her face, she hastily wiped it away with her hand. She'd felt she needed to stand up to him, but she hadn't expected their argument to get so nasty. And it bothered her that he seemed to have formed such a low opinion of her, accusing her of trying to manipulate him with sex in order to stay married to him for his money. She'd thought he respected her, but now...

Oh, the hell with him! she told herself, blinking back more tears. He was a man—what could she expect? There were no knights in shining armor. They only existed in mythology. Why did she keep hoping she'd find one?

Tira came into the kitchen then and let out a huge, long yowl. Cheri bent down to stroke the cat. "What's wrong?'' she asked. The little feline brushed against her knees and kept on yowling. She seemed agitated and distressed.

Cheri stood up again and studied Tira worriedly, wondering what was the matter. Dude ambled into the kitchen from the living room, where she'd seen him sleeping. He began sniffing Tira. Cheri was afraid they'd get into one of their usual little hissing spats, but instead, Dude seemed monumentally curious. All at once, he jumped on top of Tira.

Seeing the big black-and-white cat flattening her pet, she yelled sharply, "Dude, get off!"

"What's going on?"

Cheri turned to see Jake back in the kitchen, rolling up the long sleeves of a fresh shirt he'd tucked into jeans. "Dude's squashing my kitty!" she said. "What's the matter with him?"

Jake studied the cats, looking nettled. "Is your cat fixed?" he asked Cheri.

"No, she's too little."

Jake clapped his hands loudly. Dude responded by jumping away. Tira, however, kept on meowing. Jake shooed Dude back into the living room.

When he faced Cheri again, his voice was impatient. "Your cat's in heat. You'll have to get her spayed."

"What?"

"Don't you know anything about cats? She's in heat," he repeated. "She's even got Dude trying to mate with her. I didn't know he had it in him—he's been neutered, for Pete's sake!"

Cheri had never had a cat before and only vaguely knew what "in heat" meant. "If he's been fixed, she won't have kittens, right? So why do I have to get her spayed?" she asked with concern. "Isn't that like a hysterectomy? It's a big operation."

"Not for a cat. It's routine. Veterinarians do them all the time. Do you want to listen to her meow like this day after day? Do you want her to drive poor old Dude crazy?"

Cheri began to wonder if Jake didn't share some common ground with his cat. At least his cat, though unequipped, was willing to give lovemaking a try!

She reigned in her ironic train of thought. "But she's too little to have surgery," she said, still concerned about Tira.

"If she's old enough to be in heat, she must be old enough to be spayed. How old was she when you got her?"

"She was a stray. I have no idea where she came from or when she was born."

"Call the Millers and see if they can find a recommendation for a good vet," Jake said, reverting to his professorial, directive manner. "Arrange for Pulse to pick her up the next time he flies in with supplies. He'll probably be willing to drop her off for you at the vet. Just give him an extra piece of cake."

Jake's impatient attitude stung Cheri. He was showing his true colors now! She thought he must be the most unfeeling man she'd ever met. How had she ever thought for even one second that he was attractive?

"But she'll be scared being taken off like that," she said, her voice breaking. "We don't have any tranquilizer to give her."

Jake raised his forefinger at her. "Don't cry! You treat that cat like it was your baby. She'll survive. It's just a short plane flight and then a short car ride. She's going to be a lot more stressed for a lot longer if you don't get her fixed. So will we!" With that, he stomped out of the house.

She went to the door and called after him as he walked toward the toolshed, "I used to think you were halfway decent—for a *man*. But you're an insensitive, self-centered oaf, just like all the rest!"

He turned and looked at her. For an instant she thought he was going to say something, maybe answer her back. Instead he bowed his head and then continued walking toward the shed.

Hours later, when she brought him a sandwich for lunch, she said stiffly, "I'm sorry I called you a self-centered oaf."

He nodded as he sat at his computer, but he didn't look at her. His eyes fixed on the blue computer screen, he said in a polite, stern tone, "That's okay. I'm sorry I got angry. You still have to get your cat spayed, though."

"I know. I'll call the Millers about finding a vet."

"Good."

She left and went back into the kitchen to eat her own lunch, though she wasn't very hungry. Their year on the island had started out in such a promising way. But little by little, things had eroded between her and Jake. Now they had a hard time simply talking to each other. Jake's comment that first day had been right—it was going to be a *long* year.

Jake looked out the living-room window a few days later and saw Pulse's seaplane landing on the water. He went into the kitchen.

"Pulse is here, Cheri. You'd better put Tira into her carrier." At his insistence, Cheri had made arrangements to have her cat transported to a veterinarian in Anacortes.

Cheri was standing at the sink. A look of anxiety came into her face. "All right."

He noted what she was wearing today—pink denim pants and a tie-died, pink T-shirt that clung sublimely to every curve. "Maybe you ought to throw on a sweatshirt. You'll be going outside, and it's a little cool this morning." He gave her this advice more because he knew Pulse would all but drool if he saw her in that T-shirt than because of the outside temperature. She probably knew it, too.

Jake was a little surprised that she actually went into her room and came back out wearing one of her bulky sweatshirts. He'd gotten used to her openly disregarding his views. It indicated that perhaps her rebellion against men was aimed mostly at him.

When he saw Pulse stepping onto the pier from his small plane, Jake went down the flagstone path to meet him. Cheri came out, too.

As usual, Pulse gave her a hearty greeting and basically chatted her up as they walked back toward the house together carrying boxes of goods. Jake followed behind them, hauling plastic shopping bags full of groceries.

Once in the house, Cheri cut a piece of apple pie for Pulse and gave him a cup of coffee. The pilot sat down at the table and ate, carrying on a cheerful conversation.

"Terrific pie! How come you aren't getting fat, Jake?"

"I jog every day," Jake responded with taut patience. His dislike for the airborn Casanova had only increased with time.

Pulse glanced at Cheri. "So, I'm supposed to take your kitty-cat here to the vet?" He pointed to the brown cat sitting warily in its carrier on the floor.

Cheri paused as she put things away in the refrigerator. "Yes." She closed the fridge door and walked up to the table. "If she starts to get scared and trembles, would you open the door and pet her? She doesn't scratch, except by accident, and I clipped her claws yesterday. I don't have any tranquilizer to give her and—"

Pulse reached out and grabbed her hand. He gave it a squeeze and said, "Of course I will, and I won't mind if she does scratch."

"It might calm her down if you pet her."

"I'm sure it would. Now don't you worry one bit. I'll take good care of her."

As Pulse continued to hold her hand, Jake grew increasingly annoyed. He wished Cheri would get away from him. "You forgot to put the apples in the fridge," he reminded her.

"You can put them in the fruit and vegetable drawer," she told Jake, sounding distracted. She faced Pulse again. "So when you land, you're taking her to the vet yourself?"

"Yup."

"She won't be left alone anywhere, waiting for someone to pick her up?"

"No way would I leave her alone, Cheri," he insisted with a tender tone in his voice that sounded totally phony to Jake. But judging by her relieved expression, Cheri seemed to be buying it.

"Thank you," she said with sincerity. "I know it's silly to worry about a cat this way."

"Who says it's silly?" Pulse said in a sympathetic tone.

"Jake," Cheri replied.

Jake looked up at the ceiling.

"Well, *I* think it shows what a caring person you are. That kitty obviously means a lot to you."

"You about finished with that pie, Pulse?" Jake said, leaning against the fridge.

"Yup, sure am."

"Maybe we better get the 'kitty' loaded onto the plane," Jake suggested in as pleasant a tone as he could muster.

"You bet!" Pulse said, getting up from the table.

Jake picked up the carrier by its handle. As he held it at his side, Cheri came up and knelt in front of it. Poking two fingers between the thin metal bars on the door, she tried to touch the cat.

"Be a good kitty," she said softly. "Mommy loves you."

She stood up then, and Jake noticed she had tears in her eyes. A pang of guilt made him lower his gaze. He knew she was sending her cat away for surgery at his insistence. Even though he had the conviction that all pets should be spayed or neutered so as not to produce unwanted offspring, her anxiety still made him feel like a heel.

Pulse apparently noticed her teary eyes, too. He took it as an opportunity to put his arms around her and give her a hug.

"Don't worry, honey," he said, patting her back. "I'll have your little kitty back in no time, good as new."

"Aren't you getting behind schedule, Pulse?" Jake asked, his voice taut as he spoke through clenched teeth. He wished he could give the predatory pilot a knuckle sandwich.

Pulse seemed to take the cue, letting go of Cheri. All three walked outside, down the flagstone path to the pier. After some more small talk and reassurances, Pulse loaded the cat carrier into the plane and bid them goodbye. In minutes, he took off.

Cheri said nothing and, wiping her eyes, turned and walked back to the house. Jake followed, trying to think of something to say.

When they got into the house, he told her, "I'm sorry about your cat, Cheri, but it's for the best. She'll make a better pet once she's spayed."

Cheri nodded. "I know." She walked toward the kitchen, pulling off the heavy sweatshirt. After detouring to her bedroom briefly to put it away, she came back out, tucking her T-shirt more securely into the waistband of her pants. As she did so, she automatically stuck out her chest, giving Jake an instant surge of desire below his own waistband. God, how was he going to go on living like this with her?

"By the way," she said when she'd finished tucking, "while we're having this almost-pleasant conversation, I need to ask you something."

He noted her sarcasm, but responded in a patient manner. "Ask me anything."

"Your father is coming tomorrow for your birthday."

"Right."

"So if I bake you a birthday cake, can I assume you won't take it as a come-on? I don't want a repeat of the Valentine's Day episode. But your dad may think it odd if I don't bake you a cake."

Jake lifted his shoulders. "Sure, bake a cake. No need to give me any gift, though."

"I wouldn't dare," she said. "About the cake—if I write Happy Birthday, Jake on it in frosting, you won't read anything seductive into it?"

Jake exhaled. He supposed he deserved her scathing humor. "No, I won't. Thanks. I appreciate it, and I'm sure my dad will, too."

She nodded and looked a bit contrite. In a different, almost shy voice, she asked, "What kind do you like? White cake? Chocolate?"

"Chocolate, if you've got the ingredients."

"Oh, sure. And the frosting? Chocolate, too?"

"Why not?" he said with a grin.

She smiled back. "Good, I'm a chocaholic, too."

Jake had the urge to go over and give her a hug, as Pulse had, just because she looked so sweet. But he knew that if he did, the feel of her soft body would make him want more than a hug. So he said in a formal tone, "I need to get back to my computer. Are you feeling okay about your cat?"

"Yes. I'll call the vet later, just to make sure she got there okay."

"Good idea," Jake said. "So...I'll go back to work now."

She studied him with a faintly wry look in her pink-rimmed eyes. "You do that. I'll bring you a sandwich at noon."

* * *

As Jasper sat in the seaplane's front passenger seat next to Ken Pulsifer, he looked down at the beauty of Puget Sound on a sunny day. Far below in the distance he could see the small chain of the San Juan Islands.

"So, you've been flying in supplies for my son and daughter-in-law," he said to the pilot, hoping to glean some information. He had to raise his voice quite a bit to be heard above the roar of the engines.

"Yes, sir. She's a very sweet young woman, Cheri is. Just like Elsie Miller, she always gives me a piece of homemade dessert. Between you and me, I think Cheri is the better cook! Not that I could ever complain about Elsie's pie. But Cheri seems to have just the right touch, you know?"

"Really? Well, I'm flying in because it's my son's birthday. I'm looking forward to having an early dinner with them. I'll bring you a piece of birthday cake when you fly me back tonight."

"I'll appreciate it, Mr. Derring!"

"And…" Jasper paused, considering how to couch his question. "How do they seem to be doing? You know, they're newlyweds, and parents like me always worry. Do they seem happy to you?"

The pilot cleared his throat and seemed to hesitate.

"Please speak freely, Mr. Pulsifer. It's just between us, like your opinion of Elsie's cooking."

"All right. Actually, I have the feeling there's some tension there."

"You don't say."

"I'm afraid so. She's a real sweet, caring sort of girl, and I don't think Jake entirely appreciates what he's got. Sorry to speak ill of your son—"

"No, no. I want you to be honest. Believe me, I'm aware of my son's lack of appreciation. What makes you think so?"

"For example, the other day they asked me to take her cat to a vet in Anacortes to be fixed. She was all broken up about it, and Jake . . . well, he seemed kind of unsympathetic. So I gave her a little hug myself, just to make her feel better. Seemed to me the Christian thing to do."

Jasper smiled to himself. He knew Pulsifer had a reputation with women, which was why he hadn't been unhappy to have the pilot continue supply runs to the island after Jake and Cheri moved there. He'd hoped another man "appreciating" Jake's new wife might make his son take more notice of her, even make him jealous.

"It was good of you to comfort her," Jasper said. "Did Jake have any reaction?"

"He hurried me off, reminding me of my flight schedule. He's always polite, your son is. I'll say that."

"I know," Jasper murmured with a sigh. He'd hoped being alone with Cheri on an island would turn his cerebral son into a primal wild man. But it sounded as though the transformation hadn't taken place yet.

Jasper felt rather anxious, to tell the truth, about visiting them. He hoped his matchmaking plan was working, for their sake and also so that one day he'd have more grandchildren to brag about. And lastly, but certainly not least, he wanted to prove to Bea that he'd been right to change that clause in his will.

The island was in sight ahead of them. Jasper watched the pilot maneuver the plane into a smooth landing on the water. Soon they were at the pier, and Jake ran out to help Pulsifer tie up the small aircraft so Jasper could disembark.

He got out with the assistance of both younger men. The pilot got back in the plane then, promising to return at 7:00 p.m. to pick him up again.

As the plane took off, Jasper shook hands with Jake.

"Good to see you. Hair's getting long!" Jasper noted.

"No barbers on the island," Jake said with a laugh. "I'll have to fly to Anacortes one of these days and get a haircut."

"Have Cheri cut it," Jasper suggested as they headed up the flagstone path toward the house. "She can probably do a good-enough job while you're here on the island."

Jake drew in a breath and nodded politely. "That's an idea."

Jasper could see he didn't think it was a *good* idea. Now why might that be? Jasper wondered, hoping the answer was that Jake was strictly avoiding close physical contact with Cheri because he found her too tempting.

On the other hand, maybe Jake just wasn't attracted to her. Jasper couldn't wait to see Cheri, note her demeanor, and most of all, observe how they got on together. He guessed they'd be on good behavior in front of him. But he was always adept at sensing undercurrents. And if his youngest son didn't have any strong undercurrents by now, then thirty years ago, Bea must have found him under a cabbage leaf!

Jake opened the front door for Jasper. Cheri hurried out from the kitchen where she'd been cooking. As he watched his father and Cheri hug each other warmly, Jake felt uneasy. They were acting as if they actually were members of a family. Didn't either of them recall that this was only a temporary marriage for the convenience of fulfilling Jasper's will? Didn't his father remember his offer to pay her a million dollars? Why were they treating this as if it were real?

"Have a seat in the living room," Jake said dutifully after the two had let go of one another. "Cheri's probably got some iced tea or something."

"Yes, or lemonade," Cheri suggested. "Or would you prefer hot tea? I had some herbal tea shipped in, like you used to order at Tucci's."

"How thoughtful. I'll have that."

"How's Bea?" she asked. "It's too bad she couldn't come."

"She's just fine," Jasper said as they all strolled together into the living room. "But even flights on 747s bother her, so she wouldn't like the small planes necessary to reach the island. I promised that we'd call her today."

"That'll be fun," Cheri said.

Jake had to marvel at the way they chattered with each other. Why didn't Jasper just adopt her as another daughter and leave Jake out of it?

Jasper was studying her with shining eyes. "Life here suits you! You've gotten a bit of sun, haven't you? Not so pale as you were in Chicago. And what a lovely outfit!"

Cheri smiled and looked down at her aqua pantsuit. "Thanks. I got it from a catalog."

"Doesn't she look stunning, Jake?"

"Stunning," Jake replied. "Have a seat. How about that tea, Cheri?"

"Right away," she said. Jake felt relieved to have her out of the room.

She did look fantastic in her new outfit. Without Jake's even asking, she'd explained that she'd wanted to dress up for Jasper's visit. By now, Jake knew better than to try to convince her that she didn't have to. She had a comeback for everything, that one!

Now he had his nosy father on his hands for a few hours. He knew his dad would be watching them closely, wondering what was going on between them. And what was going on confounded Jake. Sometimes he felt almost ready and willing to chuck everything and fly back to Madison. But his research was going well, when he could keep his mind on it. Actually, Jake rather enjoyed the island itself. It was like an idyllic working vacation.

If only he didn't have to live under the same roof with a sprightly, sexy young woman, who, he suspected, wanted *him*. Other men would probably think he was completely crazy for resisting this situation, but Jake had his principles. If it was just he and Cheri, and they had met on their own with no one pulling any strings, well...maybe it might have been different. But Jasper wanted grandchildren, Cheri needed money and Jake felt he was being manipulated by them both! What man would let himself fall into such a trap? Jake's conscience, as ever, was his guide, and he would not let himself be compromised by lust. He had to resist—even if it killed him.

He sat in the living room and talked with his father for a while about his health, his trip to San Francisco, about other members of the family. Jasper went on at length about granddaughter Leslie Ann and how happy Jenny and Charles were. Cheri brought in the tea, and then excused herself to go back to the kitchen to cook. After a while, Jake took Jasper around the house and grounds, showing him his meteorologic equipment, and then to the garden, which was popping up with rows of fledgling plants.

Jake suggested that the island was so ideal, Jasper might want to rekindle his notion of making it into a private resort. To this his father replied, "But if you're so happy here, you might want to keep it for yourselves, as a vacation home."

Jake took a long breath. "Dad, Cheri and I both want to be single again when the year is up. Don't hold on to some idea that this is going to turn into a lasting marriage, because it's not!"

Jasper raised his right hand, palm out. "Whatever you say, Son. I'm not here to interfere, just to have dinner and celebrate your birthday."

Yeah, right, Jake thought to himself.

"So you're thirty already. Do you have a sense of time going faster? People do as they get older."

"Not a bit," Jake promptly replied. "I've spent so many years being younger than everyone else, it's nice to feel I'm finally at an age that has some consequence. But even so," he hastened to add, "thirty still sounds pretty young to me. I haven't even found a gray hair yet! I've got lots of years ahead to accomplish all the life goals I've set for myself—alone."

"Sounds lonely to me," Jasper said. "But you know what you want."

They sat down at the table for an early dinner at about 5:00 p.m. Cheri had made salmon baked with honey, new potatoes and a salad. Jasper complimented her heartily. Jake took the opportunity to say, "Cheri's going to have the best little café in Chicagoland, won't she?"

Jasper merely smiled as he continued chewing.

"She's been using the time here to practice different dishes, and I'm getting to sample them," Jake added, trying to be congenial. He glanced at Cheri, but she kept eating and gave no indication she'd heard him.

"How are your cats?" Jasper asked. "I saw Dude sleeping in the living room. Where's yours, Cheri?"

"She . . . you know . . . she went into heat," Cheri told Jasper with a trace of embarrassment. "She was meowing all the time and Dude was trying to mate with her—"

Jasper laughed with gusto. "My goodness! Dude? When we'd visit Jake in Wisconsin, all he ever did was sleep. So he's been awakened!"

Cheri laughed, too. "It was funny. He didn't seem to quite understand how to go about it."

"No one to show him the ropes," Jasper quipped.

Knowing his father's humor, Jake sensed this barb was aimed at him. He felt anger rising up his throat, but he went on obliviously cutting up a potato.

"So Jake said—suggested," Cheri corrected, "that I should send Tira off to have her spayed. She's at a vet in Anacortes now. She's had the operation, and she's fine."

"Cheri gets daily bulletins from the vet," Jake said, still feeling prickly.

"Well, I just want to know how she is."

"Of course," Jasper said. "When will she come home?"

Cheri sighed. "Not for a couple of weeks. She has stitches that have to come out in about ten days, so Jake said rather than fly her back and forth, we should just leave her there."

"Is that what you wanted?" Jasper asked.

"I would rather that she came home, but Jake was right. Flying so much might upset her."

Jasper smiled. "Cheri, just because you're married to Jake doesn't mean you have to be so agreeable to everything he wants. You can make your own demands."

"What makes you think she doesn't?" Jake asked in an arch tone. He glanced at Cheri. "And you never said you wanted her to come back right after the surgery."

Cheri looked self-conscious, as if not wanting to argue in front of Jasper. "It was how you suggested we do it, so—"

"You could have told me you wanted her to come back in between," Jake persisted.

"But then Pulse would have had to pick her up, bring her here, then later take her back and forth again," Cheri said, sounding slightly testy herself. "I know you don't like him, so I figured it was best to minimize the number of times we'd have to have him do us favors."

A new light gleamed in Jasper's dark eyes. "You don't like Mr. Pulsifer?"

"He's a good pilot, but he doesn't have much in the way of scruples," Jake said, pushing his last bite of salmon around his plate in an agitated way.

"Really?" Jasper said, taking on a serious tone. "How do you mean?"

"Well, Cheri and I are legally married, and for all he knows, it's a regular marriage. But he takes every opportunity to ogle her and even touch her—in front of *me*. He's got no sense of propriety."

"Oh, dear," Jasper said. "That's too bad. But I've observed Cheri waitressing at Tucci's, and I know she can hold her own with such men."

Jake looked up from his plate. "She can?" He laughed. "Could have fooled me!"

"What do you mean?" Cheri asked, her eyes directed intently at Jake.

"You let him squeeze your hand, give you hugs—"

"He hugged me *once*, because I was crying about my cat. At least he had some sympathy, which is a lot more than I can say for you," she retorted in a cool voice.

"You weren't always so accepting of him," Jake reminded her. "I remember that look you gave me when he was coming on to you in the seaplane the day he flew us here."

"Oh, you finally figured out why I gave you that look," Cheri said with amusement. "Hindsight is twenty-twenty."

"What's that supposed to mean?" Jake asked.

"At the time I gave you that telling look, on our wedding day, no less, you didn't have a clue what I was upset about. Too busy studying cloud formations! I had to handle Pulse on my own. Since then, he's actually toned down a lot—at least as far as the sort of things he says to me. He's almost a gentleman now."

Jake stared at her. "Toned down? What did he say to you the day we flew in?"

Cheri rolled her eyes. "Never mind."

"I want to know," Jake insisted.

"Why?" she asked him sharply. "Like you *care?*"

Suddenly her angry face grew self-conscious and she glanced at his father. "Sorry, Jasper. We've hit on a bone of contention." She tried to smile. "It's no big deal. Pulse only comes once a week."

"Don't be embarrassed," Jasper said with an easy smile. "This reminds me of when Bea and I were first married. Newlyweds always bicker."

"Particularly newlyweds who get married for convenience!" Jake muttered bitingly.

Jake could see the excited lights playing in Jasper's eager eyes, as if his dad was drawing the conclusion that there was more going on between him and Cheri than they were showing. Now Jake grew angry with himself. Why had he gotten into an argument with her about Pulse? It apparently had led Jasper to conclude that he was jealous of the pilot. Ridiculous! He just despised the man for being what he was, not because he was after Cheri. *Newlyweds always bicker!*

"If everyone is finished, I'll clear the dishes and get the cake," Cheri said in a light tone that sounded a bit artificial.

That was another thing, Jake thought. Why was *she* mad at him? And why wouldn't she tell him what Pulse had said?

In a minute, Cheri brought a chocolate cake to the table, aflame with thirty candles. Looking at the small bonfire, Jake did feel older.

She placed it in front of him, and Jasper and she sang "Happy Birthday." He was about to blow out the candles, but she said, "Make a wish first."

Jake looked askance. Traditions were so trite. What the hell did he have to wish for?

Let me get through this year without losing myself. The words just came to him, forming in his mind out of nowhere. Sounded good enough. He blew out the candles in one breath.

Cheri walked around the table to get a spatula and knife, then stood at his side holding them in her hand. "You want to cut it?"

He felt her feminine presence so near his shoulder. She rarely got in such close proximity to him. He had a slightly swimming feeling, smelling traces of fragrant shampoo or soap, sensing her soft essence.

"I'm not good at cutting cakes. You do it," he said. "Take it to your side of the table—there's more room."

Without a word, she picked up the cake and walked back to her chair with it.

"Looks delicious," Jasper said. "Nice writing," he added, pointing to the Happy Birthday, Jake she'd written on the frosting in white syrup.

"Can you have a piece?" she asked Jasper. "I don't suppose cake is on your stringent diet. Maybe a little one?"

"Just a sliver."

Cheri cut him a thin slice, then a thicker one for Jake. Soon they were all quietly eating cake and having coffee. Jake hoped their little, unexpected tempest had safely blown over.

But then Jasper said apologetically, "By the way, Cheri, I did promise Mr. Pulsifer I'd bring him a piece of cake on my way back. I'd let it slip that I was coming in for Jake's birthday."

"Sure," Cheri said. "I'll wrap it up for him."

"It's all right with you, Jake?" Jasper said in his most deferential manner. "I didn't realize you had such strong feelings about him."

Jake gripped his fork more tightly as he cut another bite of his cake, trying to keep his cool. He sensed his father was having a high old time trying to make him lose it by hinting he was jealous. "You can give the guy a piece of cake."

"No cherry on it though, eh?" Jasper quipped.

Cheri laughed, apparently enjoying his play on her name.

"Funny, Dad. That's a good one," Jake said, his patience sorely tried.

"*I* thought so," Jasper said, laughing.

Jake suddenly felt very weary of the whole scene. "Look, Dad, you can make your jokes and harbor your hopes about this 'marriage,' but the truth is, it's already not working out well—as you can plainly see. Cheri seems to want to put on a good front for you, but at this point I don't give a damn. Sorry to disappoint you."

Jasper's forehead creased with concern. "Don't give a damn? But...you'll stay out the year here, so you can fulfill the stipulation in my will? And finish your research project and earn your department $500,000?"

Jake exhaled in a tired manner. "Yeah, you've got me stuck here. I don't want to blow all that. And Cheri needs the money you promised her."

Jasper looked at Cheri. "What about you? Are you terribly unhappy?"

She hesitated, her expression sad and thoughtful. "No, not *terribly* unhappy. I'm accomplishing a lot on my own, like Jake. If he's willing to stick out the year, then I will, too. There's nothing for me to go back to in Chicago right now."

"I'm sorry," Jasper said, appearing and sounding contrite. The corners of his bushy eyebrows drew together over his nose. "Perhaps I've made a mistake. I admit that Bea thought it was all a bad idea. But it *is* a little too late to back out now, since everything is in motion. I'm glad you're willing to see it through. In the end, you'll both come out ahead. Keep that in mind.''

"All right," Jake said, calmer now that he'd expressed his pent-up anger. "But I hope you'll learn from this. You can't manipulate people's lives this way. You can't go around arranging marriages and expect them to work out. I know Charles and Jenny came out okay, but that was just a fluke. Cheri and I...weren't meant to be.''

Jasper looked positively grave now. Cheri kept her eyes lowered and said nothing. Jake wondered what she was thinking. He knew she must agree, however. There was nothing but constant tension between them. And she always claimed she wanted to be single.

"I'm very sorry if I've caused you two distress," Jasper said, his hand shaking slightly as he wiped his eye.

Cheri looked up. "Don't worry. We'll get used to each other— I mean, enough to get along for the rest of the year, anyway. Don't be upset, Jasper. Please..."

"You okay, Dad?" Jake said. He'd never seen his father near tears before.

"I'm fine. I'm just disappointed in myself for putting you two in this situation.''

Jake was surprised at his father's apparent contrition. Perhaps he'd finally learned his lesson. "We're tough, Dad. Don't sweat it. I know you meant well.''

Jasper nodded and seemed to regain some composure. In a little while he phoned Bea and then put Jake on the phone. Jake took on a brighter tone for his mom. Cheri did the same, when it came her turn to say hello.

At 7:00 p.m., the seaplane reappeared as scheduled. They walked with Jasper down the flagstone path to the pier. Cheri had wrapped a piece of cake in foil for him to give to Pulse. There was a sense of anticlimax as they said goodbye.

Walking back toward the house as the plane flew off in the distance, Jake said to Cheri, "Thanks for the dinner and the cake. It was great."

"That's all right. You were brutally honest with him," she said. "He's an old man and in fragile health, Jake. Maybe what you said was true, but—"

"I should have been gentler? Maybe. But Dad gets so set on his ideas, I felt I had to make sure he understood we have different ideas."

"So...about us," she said. "From my point of view, I was glad to hear you spell things out. You've been pretty taciturn. I wish you'd continue to be that straightforward instead of keeping things to yourself. I like to know where I stand with you."

Jake was surprised. "Okay. I will." Though he agreed, he grew nervous for some reason. "I didn't expect to get into that argument with you about Pulse."

"Neither did I."

"I'm not...jealous, or anything like that. He just bugs me, that's all."

She nodded. "I understand."

"So, what did he say to you, when he was flying us here?"

She looked up at him and squinted, as if trying to decipher him. "If you're not jealous, why do you need to know?"

Jake had no answer and let the matter drop.

As Jasper sat in the seaplane while Pulsifer flew them back to Anacortes, he felt a secret glee that he would not share with the pilot. *His plan was working!* Jasper could sense it, though he'd had to make an effort to hide his insights, even acting downright remorseful in front of them. But Jake obviously wanted Cheri. Jasper could tell by the way he'd behaved when she stood next to him with the cake. And he'd sensed that Cheri secretly wanted Jake.

Jasper chuckled to himself. It was marvelous! If those two didn't make love, and soon, they'd spontaneously combust.

7

Over a week later, Cheri glanced out the living room window with anticipation when she heard the distant buzz of a plane's engines. Pulse was scheduled to make a special trip to bring back Tira today after her stitches were removed. Cheri couldn't wait to have her little cat safely home again.

Jake came in, apparently having heard the plane, too. "I'll go out and meet him and pick up your cat. No need for you to—"

"No," she said. "I'm going out myself."

He pointedly eyed her T-shirt and shorts. The weather had turned surprisingly warm the last few days, bringing an early spring.

"Yes, I'm going like this," she told him in no uncertain terms.

Jake seemed to accept her reprimand, but he explained, "It's just the way he always ogles you. You may not even notice it."

"Jake, I know how he looks at me. But he's basically harmless and he's bringing my cat home." She glanced outside again and saw the plane skimming the surface of the water up to the pier. "Come on," she said, giving Jake an impish look, "you can be our chaperon."

"Better believe it," he muttered under his breath.

She heard his comment and smiled to herself. More and more she had the impression that Jake was all over the place in his attitudes and emotions. He acted jealous but claimed he wasn't. He gazed at her with longing, but when she caught his glance, he grew reserved and left the room. Ever since The Kiss, the poor man had been fighting his yearning for her with all he had. Cheri felt rather complimented that she could attract a man of such caliber, a scientist and professor no less, even if it was only a physical attraction. She just wondered if he would ever come down from his ivory tower and take advantage of his rights as her husband.

On the other hand, since they had no real future together, maybe it was just as well he stayed up there. She was getting a little tired of the bickering, though, the by-product of their repressed urges. Her desire for him had not abated any more than his had. Unlike him, however, she was willing to admit it—*and* do something about it.

When they reached the pier, Pulse had already gotten out of the plane and was tying it up to the wood posts. He waved to them, then reached into the back of the plane, pulling out Cheri's cat carrier.

"Look what I've got here!" he said with obvious pleasure. Cheri ran up to him. When he got a good look at her, the pleasure in his eyes changed slightly, becoming awed as opposed to merely cheerful.

Cheri ignored it, more interested in seeing her cat. Tira meowed at her through the thin metal bars. Cheri took the carrier from him, set it down on the pier and opened the door. She lifted the cat out and hugged it, noticing that the fur on the lower part of its stomach had been shaved off and there was a small scar.

"Poor kitty," she said, tears in her eyes. "You're home now."

Tira got a bit agitated, however, so Cheri put her back in the carrier, not wanting her to run off. She turned to

Pulse and held out her hand. "Thanks for taking care of her. I'm very grateful."

The pilot took her hand with an eager smile. He slid his arm around her and gave her a long squeeze. "Glad to help you out anytime. You're a sweet little lady."

All this rather amused Cheri. She was so happy that he'd brought Tira back, she couldn't be angry with him. "I've got some pie—" she began to offer.

"Um, thanks," Pulse said, letting her go suddenly, "but I have to get back to Anacortes. Got some tourists signed up for a plane ride." She noticed he was looking over her head at Jake, who she knew was standing behind her. Turning to give Jake a quick glance, she saw him glowering at the pilot. He looked surprisingly fierce, his dark brown eyes shimmering with warning lights. No wonder Pulse had so quickly decided he needed to get back to his tourists.

"Next time," she promised him.

"Right!" the pilot said. "Looking forward to it." He began edging toward his plane. Jake rushed to help him untie the aircraft. Pulse got in, avoiding eye contact with Jake. He waved at Cheri and took off.

Jake picked up the cat carrier, and they walked toward the house. She could tell he was still seething.

"Something wrong?" she asked lightly, taking a perverse delight in baiting him.

"'I'm very grateful,'" he said, imitating her. "He's got his hands all over you, and you're grateful!"

"Well, he did take good care of Tira," she said.

"Offering him pie!"

"I always do. He'd expect it. You sure scared him off in a hurry! I didn't know you had it in you."

"What's that supposed to mean?" he asked testily.

"You do a good imitation of a jealous man."

They entered the house and he set the cat carrier on the floor. He made no reply to her last comment, though she sensed he was still thinking about it.

She bent down to open the carrier door. As Tira cautiously came out, Cheri picked her up to hold her again. While nuzzling the cat in her arms, she felt Jake's eyes on her. She turned and found him standing there on the linoleum floor, glaring at her.

"What?" she said.

"You were flirting with him." His tone *sounded* matter-of-fact, but there was an edge to it.

"Oh, for crying out loud! Why, because I shook hands with him?"

"You were a lot friendlier than you needed to be."

His stern voice seemed to frighten Tira. The cat jumped out of Cheri's arms and ran from the room. "Now you've scared her!"

He looked after the cat, then back at Cheri, exasperated. "Sorry! You just get me so aggravated the way you deal with that pilot. You claim you know he ogles you, and now you're getting downright friendly with him."

"He did me a favor," she said.

"What other favors do you want from him?"

This threw her a bit. "What kind of an insinuation is that? I don't want anything from him."

"I wouldn't think so. But ever since that kiss, you've struck me as being on the prowl. You don't dress demurely anymore, and you gaze at me with that—that *look* in your eyes!"

"What look?" she asked.

"Like you want to continue where the kiss left off," he said, his eyes pinning hers.

She thought a moment about how to answer. Might as well be honest. "Maybe I do," she said, wondering how he would respond.

Jake's eyes widened, as if he was startled. "So why are you so friendly with Pulse? Any man will do?"

This made her angry. "Why not? *You* act like you'll get electrocuted if you even touch me."

"Is that what you want, then, to be 'touched' by a man?" He edged toward her.

She didn't back away. "I'm twenty-three and healthy. I have needs like any other woman."

"So you're taking any man at hand?" he asked in an interrogative tone, still moving toward her.

"No."

"You're being selective?"

"Yes." Her heart was beginning to beat faster.

"You're selecting Pulse."

"No."

"No?" His voice grew ominously soft. "That leaves only me."

"You're good at subtraction," she said, excited, a little scared, relishing toughing him out.

"But you once told me quite clearly that you'd never be interested in going to bed with me."

She stared into his alert, shining eyes, but remained silent, waiting.

"Didn't you say that?" he repeated.

"Yes."

"Well?"

"I was mistaken," she said quietly.

A dark flash in his eyes grew into a flame. "You really are turning yourself into a little seductress, aren't you? I warned you. I'm only human. You should be careful what you wish for—you might get it!"

Her eyes grew wide. Did he mean . . . ? "What are you saying?" she whispered.

"That I can't stand this anymore. If you keep taunting me with that pilot, if you keep flaunting yourself around me, keep on behaving like you're hungry for sex, then that's what you'll get.''

''Is that a promise?'' she asked, shaking.

He was in her face now, almost nose-to-nose. ''You're seducing me! Admit it.''

''Trying to,'' she said. ''It's not like I've had lots of practice.'' She swallowed. ''Am I succeeding?''

A vertical crease formed in his forehead and he looked helplessly confused. ''Damn you, you throw me every time. I never met anyone like you!''

''What? How?'' she asked, wondering if she'd somehow blown her chance, destroyed the moment of opportunity.

''You're so damned adorable! Right now I want to hold you and reassure you. A moment ago I was ready to carry you into the bedroom.''

She smiled hesitantly. ''You think I'm adorable?''

His expression changed. ''Never mind that,'' he told her, as if he wished he hadn't said it.

''Okay,'' she readily agreed. ''Then let's get back to the part about you wanting to carry me into the bedroom.''

His eyes became glazed as he stared at her. ''I think about that at least five times an hour.''

''So do I.''

A half second of silence hung between them. ''You do?'' he said.

''Yes.'' She stared at him, waiting. He merely stared back. The suspense was driving her crazy. ''We are legally married, Jake. It's not like we'd be doing anything illicit.''

''It would shatter all our plans.''

''Why?''

''Because it would. We'd have a heavy-duty relationship then.''

''Not necessarily,'' she argued. ''We could just do it once, you know? Just once, to see how it is, to appease our curiosity. Then we'd know what it's like and—and then—''

''We'd want to keep on doing it,'' he said.

''We would?''

His eyes narrowed. ''You really are innocent, aren't you?''

She bowed her head. ''Yes.'' Looking up, she said, ''That's why I—I want you to be the first. I . . . feel safe with you. I'm attracted to you. We're married—for the time being, anyway. Why not do it? Why not take me to bed, Jake?''

''Sex can change everything—how we look upon each other, what we think about, what we do. There's no going back, Cheri.''

''It's not particularly pleasant the way it's been. It might be a change for the good. It would ease the tension. We might stop bickering so much. We've got to do *some*thing,'' she said, tilting her chin up.

His eyes focused on her mouth. ''I want you so much, I can't think straight anymore.'' His voice had grown husky and low. She felt his warm hand slide upward over her breast. ''You're so desirable,'' he whispered roughly, then kissed her hotly on the mouth.

Her head swam with joy. As she kissed him back eagerly, she began unbuttoning his shirt. He broke the kiss to rip off the shirt. He tore off his glasses and tossed them on the kitchen table. Cheri did not hesitate. She pulled her T-shirt up over her head and threw it aside. Reaching in back, she unhooked her bra and let it slide down her arms to the floor. He gazed at her in absorbed reverence. For once, she was proud of her body. Smiling, she stepped forward and pressed her breasts softly against his bared chest.

Making an urgent sound in his throat, he took her in his arms and kissed her shoulder, then gently pushed her breast upward with his hand and kissed her plumped flesh. She whimpered softly, then gasped with heightening pleasure as she felt him test her nipple with his teeth.

All at once she felt his arm come under her knees, and he lifted her up into his arms. She slid her hands around his neck and kissed his face and hair as he carried her into his bedroom. He laid her on the bed and quickly went to work on the button of her shorts. He slid the shorts, along with her panties, off her body. She'd never been nude in front of a man before and instinctively bent her knee and slid her thigh upward to hide herself.

After tossing aside her clothes, he unzipped his pants. In a second, he also was nude. She involuntarily drew in a sharp breath as she saw his taut arousal.

"It won't fit," she whispered with wonder as he moved toward her, lowering himself onto the bed over her.

She felt his body shake with laughter. He looked down at her, smiling broadly. "It'll fit." His expression sobered a bit. "It might hurt at first though, because you're a virgin."

She nodded. "I've heard that. Were the other women you've known virgins?"

"No. This will be a new experience for both of us." He gazed at her intently. "I'm a little nervous."

She gave him a shaky grin. "I'll be gentle with you."

He smiled again. "You and your sassy quips. You aren't supposed to outwit me so much—*I'm* the professor."

She ran her hands over his pectoral muscles, feeling his chest hair between her fingers, touching his nipples as he loomed over her. "So teach me something."

His eyes closed tightly with urgent need as he kissed her mouth, then her breasts. He caressed her all the while he kissed her flesh, and the way he handled her body was so ardent, yet cherishing, that her eyes began to fill with tears. She'd been longing for the right man to touch her this way for years. And now he was finally here, giving her what she'd craved in her heart for so long.

"Oh, Jake," she whispered as a tear slid back into her hair, "You can do this to me forever."

His mouth left her breasts and came back to her lips. He seemed to be chuckling as he kissed her. "I can't last that long."

Her heart beat fast. "Then do what you want," she told him in a hushed voice.

He gazed appreciatively into her eyes, and while he held her gaze, she felt his hand slide downward from her breast, over her stomach. Her mouth opened in a startled gasp as his fingers slipped between her closed thighs. He swiftly found her body's most sensitive spot, which had become surprisingly slick. And then a marvelous wave of electricity sped through her limbs and made her breath come faster. She parted her thighs. "Ohh, Jake!"

"You're so aroused," he said with wonder. "So soon. You're ready, aren't you?"

She didn't know exactly what he meant, but what he was doing to her with his dextrous fingers was driving her so wild, she'd begun writhing on the pillow. She could hardly breathe, her heart was pounding so fast, and her mind was totally focused on that part of her body he was attending to with such expertise. "Jake, you're making me go out of my mind." Instinctively, she bent her knees and her hips began to undulate, wanting to assuage the ache inside her. "Is it supposed to be like this?" she asked, her voice breaking with need.

"Yes," he whispered. "But it so rarely is. You're going to be a dream lover." He moved over her, lowering himself between her thighs. With his hand, he guided his member into her warm femininity. She felt the thick length of him sliding into her. It seemed intrusive and odd, and then it hurt. She whimpered in pain.

Jake stopped moving. "Are you all right?"

"Yes. It's okay, Jake," she said, earnestly looking into his eyes, wanting to be brave. "I want to do this."

Gently, he moved within her again, entering her completely. She smiled at him tentatively as another tear rolled back into her hair. "It doesn't hurt anymore," she whispered. "Go ahead."

He kissed her mouth and murmured, "You're the sweetest, sexiest, most adorable woman. I've been trying not to fantasize about you for weeks. And this is so much better than any fantasy...." He kissed her more aggressively as she clung to him tightly, her arms around his back.

The aching within her had been appeased now that they were one, and she felt sublimely whole. But as he slowly began to move back and forth inside her, the aching returned almost instantly. Instinctively she brought her legs up over his buttocks, and she arched her head back as he kissed her throat.

Soon she began to gasp with each forward thrust and pant audibly each time he ground his pelvis against hers. Her forehead broke out in perspiration as she writhed with aching pleasure, her body in tandem with his in an ever-heightening, pulsating rhythm.

All at once she felt a change in her body, in the tension below her belly button. A high, singing gasp of wonder escaped her as she felt transcended, suspended for a moment. And suddenly she gave a little cry as her body broke into convulsions of torrid pleasure.

After the intense physical release, which stunned her mind and left her breathless, she relaxed and sighed, while Jake continued to grip her tightly. His body grew taut and she could feel him pulsating within her.

And she realized with a sudden little shock that his semen must be inside her. That was what this exquisite bliss was really all about—procreation. She'd sort of forgotten. He'd been so resistant until now, she hadn't seen any need to protect herself. And when he'd come toward her with his urgent, fiery eyes, all she'd thought about was experiencing what she longed for with the man she'd come to long for.

How likely was it that she'd get pregnant the first time? She decided she wasn't going to worry about it. Their lovemaking had been too glorious to spoil it with concern about something that might never happen.

Jake moved off of her and settled close at her side. Still breathing heavily, he kissed her hair as she snuggled beside him. He ran the heel of his hand over his damp forehead. "I didn't know it could be like that. I reached some metaphysical plateau I didn't know existed."

Cheri sighed and ran her hand over his chest. "You were wonderful, Jake. You made the first time exquisite for me." Tears filled her eyes. She realized she was almost ready to tell him she loved him. Instead she lay her head on his shoulder, feeling confused.

"It didn't hurt too much?" he asked, running his hand over her arm.

"No. It was...like a peek at heaven," she said, her chin starting to tremble. With her head on his shoulder, he couldn't see her face. She was glad he couldn't, afraid her emotion might disturb him. She wanted him to be happy about their experience—because she didn't want it to end. The realization was gradually becoming clear to her that she was indeed falling in love with Jake. Oh, God, she thought. What now?

A peek at heaven, Jake repeated to himself as he stroked her soft skin. What an apt way to put it. He'd never thought sex could be so—so spiritual. She'd brought out something in him he didn't know was there. He knew he'd want to experience it again...and again.

But that created a problem, he realized as his body recovered its equilibrium and he regained his focus. It was

the very problem he'd foreseen and warned her about—
that once they started, they wouldn't want to stop. He
had the feeling she didn't care, didn't think about the
future or what they were getting into. She was impulsive. And now she'd made him impulsive, too—at least
she'd made him give in to his raging desire. Maybe giving in had been inevitable.

But what now? he worried. He'd gotten himself more
deeply enmeshed in their situation. His desire had made
his plans go awry. What happened next? What should he
do about getting himself back on track?

8

━━━▶◀━━━

That evening, Cheri called Jake for dinner as usual. After they'd gotten out of bed earlier in the day, they'd kissed, and then gone about their usual daily routines. Hours had passed now, and Cheri wondered how Jake would behave toward her. Would he have regrets about their lovemaking?

He came in and sat down. When she placed the main dish, Hungarian stuffed green peppers, on the table, he smiled and told her it smelled good. His reaction gave Cheri a feeling of relief. She was afraid he might be uptight again and start accusing her of seducing him, as he had before.

She sat down at the table with him and served him portions of food. As they began to eat, she said, "I don't know about you, but I've had extra energy all day. I didn't know making love would be so invigorating!"

His demeanor changed slightly, growing more deliberate. He chewed more slowly and kept his eyes on his plate. When he'd swallowed, he said, "I know what we shared earlier was a memorable experience, but we're going to have to look upon it as an isolated incident."

She lowered her fork. "What do you mean?"

"I mean, I think we need to make a vow to each other that it won't happen again."

His statement made her heart plummet. "Why?"

"I think we've lost track of our original goals. We were both using this opportunity, contrived for all the wrong reasons by my father, to pursue our separate careers. We promised each other *no sex,* remember?"

"Yes. But…that was then. We didn't know we'd grow attracted to each other."

He nodded grimly. "Exactly what my father was counting on. You put two lab mice in a cage, they'll mate. You throw a man and woman together on an isolated island, the same thing will happen. What my dad created here, for his own purposes, was a giant lab experiment. That we'd wind up having sex was exactly what he expected. Well, it may have happened once, but we ought to have more respect for ourselves and our goals than to let it happen again. We'd be allowing my father to win this game he's playing with our lives."

Cheri sat still and chewed her lip, not knowing what to say. Her eyes misted. She felt as if something wonderful she'd just discovered was suddenly being taken away.

Jake eyed her and seemed to sense her sadness. "Don't feel bad about it, Cheri. I'm not blaming you. I know sometimes I tried to make out that you were seducing me, but that was just an excuse I used to cover up my own dilemma. I've thought about it all afternoon, and, if anything, this is more my fault than yours. I know my father a lot better than you do. I should have been more diligent about remembering *his* motives and making sure I didn't fall into his trap."

"So what am I?" she asked. "Bait?"

His face grew sympathetic. "You're a lovely, gorgeous woman, but you're a little naive, and I'm afraid that's basically what my father did—he used you as bait to get me into a sexual liaison he hoped would stick. Remember, all he wants is grandchildren. You have the look of a young woman who would be fertile. He knew you were down on your luck and needed money, so he took advantage and figured out a way to set us up.''

Cheri vigorously shook her head. ''You talk about your father in such a negative, cynical way. I just don't see him as being as coldly manipulative as you say.''

''No, he's not cold about it. In fact, his method is to find ways to light *fires* under people. He did it to my brother, and now he's doing it to me.''

''But your brother is happily married,'' Cheri said.

''That's beside the point. It was just their good luck that they fell in love.''

Cheri read into this that Jake didn't foresee a similar turn of events happening in his life—he didn't anticipate that he would fall in love with her. A cold feeling of isolation came over her. She was all alone in her feelings of love and eager passion. To Jake, apparently, it had just been a sexual encounter they shouldn't have had. ''So you think our sleeping together was a mistake?''

He hesitated, as if searching for words. ''A beautiful mistake, but yes, it was. As I said before, we both lost sight of our goals.''

''It's nice you can see it all so intellectually.'' She tried to keep her voice from breaking.

He exhaled uneasily, as though perceiving she was upset. ''You're young and it was your first experience. The first time I had sex, I sort of lost my moorings for a few weeks and got sidetracked by indulging my physical urges. But people who allow themselves to get sidetracked that way will have a hard time staying on the path to their ultimate goal. I sense you're very bright, Cheri. Brighter than even you realize. You could probably do a lot more than run your own café. But if that's what you want, then keep that goal ahead of you, and don't get swept away by one hour of terrific sex.''

''But—but sex is normal. People need it,'' she argued. ''Can't people pursue their goals *and* have sex?''

Jake rubbed his eyes with his thumb and forefinger. "Yes, of course, but it's awfully distracting and time consuming. There are so many more important things to accomplish than to spend time fueling a relationship. A sex partner has expectations they want met, and pretty soon your life isn't your own anymore. Which brings me back to what we both stated from the beginning, that we each wanted to lead our own *single* lives. Right?"

Cheri nodded reluctantly. Yes, she had said that. She supposed he was right. He was so eloquently cerebral about it all. Damn him! "All right," she acquiesced, "if that's what you want."

"Isn't it what you want?" he asked in a tutorial manner. "Think first before you answer."

Cheri pressed her lips together. It seemed to her that *he* thought about things too much. But earlier he had finally stopped thinking. He'd acted on his desires. Perhaps it would happen again. Maybe she just needed a little patience. "I guess I want it all, Jake. I don't like making choices."

He drew his brows together, obviously not liking her reply. "But when you were engaged and going into business with your fiancé, you put sex aside *then*, didn't you?"

The question took her by surprise. She'd forgotten. But instantly she knew the reason. She hadn't been in love with her fiancé as she was with Jake. Her instincts had kept her from getting into a physical relationship with the man. Maybe on some unconscious level she didn't trust him.

But she'd do anything for Jake.

She wet her lips as she thought how to answer him. "I had a personal rule that I wanted to wait until I was married to have sex. Fortunately, I never married my fiancé. But . . . I *am* married to you."

"It's a sham marriage. We both know it's only for a year."

"But it's legal," she said. A new argument came to her. "If we have a marriage of convenience, why not have sex for convenience?"

He looked off into space for a moment, as if stumped by her logic. When he glanced at her again, she sensed it was with reluctance, or maybe trepidation. "You're that anxious to keep on having sex with me?"

"You bet! You're a wonderful lover. I want more!"

He colored at her zealous reply, but he managed to keep his composure. "That's what I warned you about, that we'd want to keep on doing it."

"So why don't we? Isn't it easier to concentrate on your work if you have your physical needs met?"

He shook his head and seemed increasingly uneasy. "I—I don't think so. I'd want to go to bed with you constantly. I wouldn't get anything done. It would completely unbalance my life."

"Did that happen with your previous relationships?"

"No. The other women I've dated understood about keeping priorities straight. It…I don't know why, it just wasn't a problem. And those relationships didn't last long. We're here together for a whole year."

"I see," she said. "And I don't share your concept about priorities, I guess."

He took a breath and cocked his head. "No, you sure don't seem to. You apparently haven't learned that yet. It comes with maturity."

"But weren't you *always* mature?" she asked. "Even before you were grown up, all you did was study and skip grades, right? So I guess you were born that way."

He chuckled to himself and pinched his nose. "You might say that. Not that I wanted to be, but you have a point. I'm beginning to see that you and I have a different basic approach to life. I set myself parameters. You set parameters, too, I think—but then you go and leap right over them."

Cheri laughed. Actually, he was right. But she'd started leaping boundary lines only after she'd met him. Jake had spun her life around, and her original goals were changing fast.

She realized, though, that she'd have to take things at Jake's pace if she was going to have any chance of reaching her new goal. He'd once accused her of wanting to stay married to him permanently—so she could be the pampered wife of a millionaire's son, he'd said. He'd been wrong—then. But now she realized it was true; she wanted to stay married to him. Not for his money or Jasper's, but because she'd fallen in love with Jake and wanted to go on living with and making love with him.

"Okay," she said. "I see where we stand. Thanks for being straightforward with me. We both need to want to continue making love, and if you're not comfortable about it, then we won't. I'll just go on pursuing my interests, and you'll do likewise with yours."

She knew that if she was going to have any hope of keeping Jake, she'd better not make him feel any more manipulated than he already felt by his father. If he came to her again, it needed to be because he wanted to of his own free will.

Jake stared at her for a moment, as if replaying in his mind what she'd said, to make sure he'd heard right. He looked relieved. "Good. I'm glad you understand. I think you'll be happy in the long run that we returned to our original agreement."

"I hope you're right," she said in a positive tone.

As they resumed eating, they began a more mundane conversation. She discussed with him what supplies they should order, how the vegetable garden was growing and that the bathroom sink was a bit stopped up. Then she asked, "How are your morning jogs? Have you ever gone all the way around the island yet?"

"No. I always go about three miles and then come back."

"I haven't, either. But I still want to. The weather's getting warmer and I want to find the small beach that's supposed to be here somewhere."

"The water would be too cold for swimming, at least until well into summer," he cautioned her.

"That's okay," she said blithely. "I'm more interested in getting a nice tan. Since we have a totally private beach, it may be the only chance I'll ever have to sunbathe nude." She noticed him pause as he cut some asparagus on his plate. "I can take my correspondence-course material with me to study while I'm laying out on the beach," she chattered on, "so I won't be losing any study time."

He nodded, kept his eyes on his plate and murmured, "Good idea."

Cheri thought about inviting him to join her sometime, but decided not to push it. She hoped he was thinking about that idea already—and worrying how he'd ever get the image of her lying nude on the sand out of his mind.

The next day she started early and walked around the entire island. She discovered that the small beach was actually not far from the house, but in the opposite direction. The trail going that way was hidden among a stand of trees on the far side of the house. Now that she knew how to find it, she could follow the trail and come to the beach in about ten minutes, walking at a comfortable pace.

At dinner that evening, she apprised Jake of her discovery and announced her intention to begin sunbathing there the next day.

* * *

From the ridge, Jake watched the weather balloon he'd just released rise into the sky carrying its box of sensors upward through the atmosphere. He'd been sending them up twice a day without fail. Picking up a pair of binoculars, he watched the balloon for a moment, then studied the cloud formations above the mountains on the western horizon.

He lowered the binoculars and looked over the island from his elevated vantage point. He couldn't see the entire island, there being high ridges to the southwest, but he could view a great deal of it. The foliage was thickening with spring weather, and he could see some wildflowers growing in a meadow below the ridge on which he was standing. Beyond that was the shoreline and the sparkling waters of Puget Sound. He thought he saw something moving, and he raised his binoculars to check.

Focusing them on the shoreline, he realized he could see a patch of beach beyond the tops of some trees. It seemed as if the sand was moving. As he refocused the binoculars, he saw the form that was moving was flesh colored. Instantly he knew it was Cheri. Long hair flowing down her bare back, she was walking along the water's edge, looking down at the sand, perhaps hunting for seashells. Her beautiful, rounded bottom was bare. She turned then, and he could see her exquisite breasts jutting out from her narrow rib cage above her small waist. She bent down to pick up something, and as she stood up again, her long hair brushed over her nipples before the breeze blew it back.

Jake felt as if he were glimpsing some lovely nymph, at one with nature and unaware of her incredible beauty. Conscious of his thoughts, he lowered the binoculars, wishing he hadn't caught that glimpse. He hadn't even known the beach was located at that spot, having never particularly looked for it. Instructing himself to forget the image he'd just seen, he began making his way back down the ridge. As he neared the bottom, he looked off into the stand of trees a little distance from the house and for the first time noticed a narrow trail that wound into the woods. He realized it must be the path Cheri had mentioned that led to the beach.

Jake found himself stopping in his tracks, despite his intention to go back into the house. No, he shouldn't go down that path between the trees. It was forbidden, off limits. If he did, then he had no willpower.

But that glimpse of Cheri had taken over his mind and his body. More than a week had gone by since that day he'd carried her into his bedroom. He'd had trouble keeping himself from remembering every erotic moment he'd shared with her, and now seeing her on the beach, looking so naked and natural, was more than he could withstand. He began to walk toward the path through the woods. With each step he told himself, *Wrong way! Don't go in this direction! You have work to get done. You have a scientific project to attend to, a career to keep on track.* But Jake didn't listen.

Soon he was deep among the trees, then the path opened out into sunshine. It led along a rocky shore for some distance, then turned inland when the shoreline formed a protected cove. There a new little trail forked off the main one. The little trail led downward to the sand beach inside the cove. He paused at the crossroads and wondered where Cheri was. And then he saw her lying on her stomach on a towel, propped up on her elbows as she read her basic-accounting textbook.

She hadn't seen or heard him. He could still go back, he told himself. But as his eyes took in her smooth skin and delightful curves, he forgot about the idea of turning back. Instead he walked down to the tiny beach.

He was about three yards from her when the soft sound of his shoes on the sand made her look up. Her eyes widened and she dropped the book. Perhaps it was instinct, but she grabbed an extra towel and covered her breasts as she sat up.

"Jake!" She laughed. "You took me by surprise."

He smiled, but didn't quite know what to say. He stuck his hands in his pockets and bowed his head.

"Are you out for a walk?" she asked.

He looked at her again. "No. I was up on the ridge and saw you through my binoculars." His heart was beginning to pound. Her long hair around her shoulders, her legs curled to one side, she looked like a sexy innocent sitting there on the big towel, clutching the smaller towel over her chest. As she pressed the terry cloth against her, she pushed her breasts upward, making plump cleavage appear. "You . . . looked so beautiful."

She smiled and glanced away, appearing almost shy. "So you came to see me?" Her winsome eyes slowly moved up to meet his. "I've been hoping you'd come out here and enjoy the beach with me. It's a nice spot."

He had the feeling she'd been waiting for him to come to her, like a fly to honey. And here he was. He'd taken the bait again. But at this point, his body was telling him not to give a damn about all that. He'd made his decision with every step he'd taken here.

"I've been dying to make love with you again," he said, his voice husky.

Her eyes took on an extra sheen and she sighed. "So have I." She lowered the towel from her breasts. "I've been dreaming about making love with you here." She lay down on her back on the towel and looked up at him with longing, holding out her arms. Her voice was a sensuous whisper. "Oh, Jake. Come to me."

As if he were in some erotic dream, he tore off his shirt and glasses, unzipped his pants and threw himself on top of her. He kissed her mouth with burning passion, fondling her breasts and settling himself between her soft thighs, eagerly parted for him. Reaching between them with his hand, he felt the slick moistness between her legs as she groaned with pleasure. His heart pounded as his throbbing member entered her. Her softness enveloping him gave such exquisite torment, he closed his eyes and nearly wept. There was no way he could keep away from her, no matter how much he tried. His priorities could go to hell. He didn't care anymore. She made him feel fully alive in some primordial way he discovered only with her.

Driven by his pounding need, he drew back and thrust hard. She arched her spine, threw back her head and cried out his name to the sky. As she writhed, her cushiony breasts rose against his chest. He squeezed her flesh with his hand and kissed her neck, while grinding his pelvis against hers.

"Am I hurting you?" he asked in a ragged whisper.

"It's all right. I've wanted this...craved this! Ohh, Jake. You're so strong, so manly...." She began to breathe in gasps while her hands on his buttocks encouraged him urgently to continue his thrusts. "Jake! Jake!" All at once she cried out as her body convulsed wildly beneath his. Her erotic reaction made him smile, knowing he was thoroughly satisfying her. His brain turned liquid and he exploded deep inside her. They clung to one another through the long, enraptured moment.

Gently they disentangled themselves, and he lay next to her, keeping her in his arms. When he'd caught his breath, he said, "I must have been delusional, thinking we could keep away from each other."

She laughed and ran her hand over his chest roughly. "I thought so."

"You *are* a seductress—a siren here on this beach! You told me you'd sunbathe here, knowing it would lure me back."

"I hoped so," she admitted. "I was beginning to wonder if you would ever come to me. I've longed for you every day."

She always freely admitted her sexual desire to him. It was refreshing in a woman, and exciting. She was like something out of some sublime fantasy come to life and here just for him. He'd be crazy to resist anymore.

"I decided you were right," he said. "Since we have a marriage of convenience, we might as well have sex for convenience."

She grinned, her eyes sparkling and alive. "Whenever we want? From now on?"

He nodded. "From now on. I'm available whenever. That suit you, you sexy, adorable beggar?"

Her eyes took on an energized yet profound light. "That suits me just fine," she whispered. "I'm so happy!"

He felt mesmerized by her sweet face for a moment. Then he said, "But there is one thing, Cheri. It wouldn't be good if you got pregnant. That would really mess up our lives. Since you were a virgin, I don't suppose you're on the pill."

"No."

"Better order some condoms from the drugstore, then."

"Okay," she said. "I will."

He stayed on the beach with her for a few blissful hours and they made love again. As they walked back to the house together later on, Jake had no regrets, no more second thoughts. He was done with that after today. Whether his father had set him up or not, he'd finally recognized that he had stumbled into paradise. He was living on his own private island with a beautiful woman who wanted him, who made him feel like a superhero. Why should he give this up? She'd asked why they couldn't pursue their studies and enjoy sex, too. Well, maybe she was right. He'd never attempted it before. But he had the feeling that if he tried hard enough, he could make it work. God, this was turning out to be a glorious year!

9

Four months later, Jake had learned that a hot sexual relationship was indeed a distraction, but he somehow managed to indulge and still get all his scientific work done. His study of the microclimate was coming along very well. He felt more content with himself and at one with nature and the world than he ever could have imagined.

Sometimes, like now, as he lay on the beach next to Cheri after making love, listening to the waves on the sand, watching fluffy cumulus clouds float across the sky, he started to think everything was too perfect. It scared him a little. In less than six months, their idyllic year on the island would be over. Whenever he thought about that seriously, he began to grow uneasy and unsettled. Would he be able to adjust to going back to his old life in Wisconsin, living alone, teaching at the university? Of course, there would be scientific expeditions to take part in, which would be exciting and rewarding. But his everyday life was going to seem unfulfilling after living on the island with Cheri.

Still, he would have to make that adjustment back to normal life when the time came. He had his goals to pursue. He couldn't let his habit of having sex with a beautiful woman whenever he wanted get in his way. Sometimes, in more erotic moments when he wasn't thinking clearly, he thought about asking Cheri to continue living with him in Madison. But his common sense told him that even if she was willing, it just wouldn't work. He was so different here with her. She'd brought out a new, untamed aspect of his personality he hadn't known was there. He'd let his hair grow long and didn't care. He went around half-dressed when he wanted, because she liked to see his chest. They had sex whenever and wherever they wanted. Sometimes all she had to do was bring him his sandwich for lunch, and they'd wind up with her astride him on the chair, in front of his blinking computer, writhing in ecstasy.

He couldn't go back to Madison, be among his academic colleagues, feeling so free and behaving like this. He'd lost all his former discipline. They would probably read in his face and demeanor that he'd become addicted to something. They might wonder if it was drugs, never guessing that quiet, hardworking Professor Derring had been mesmerized by a beautiful siren into indulging in his own longterm, private sexual fantasy.

There was no question it had to stop. He had to leave Cheri at the end of the year, as planned, or he'd never have his old life back again.

Jake knew he'd have to go through a withdrawal period. He didn't know how long it would take, because disengaging from her was going to be harder than he'd ever imagined. She'd insinuated herself into his life, maybe even into his psyche. He'd begun to think of them as a unit, a couple, rather than as separate, independent people. That had been a mistake. But it had happened before he'd realized it. Maybe it was because of their close physical relationship; they'd come to instinctively know, even without talking, what would please the other while their bodies were entwined. Such an intimate physical bond was seductive and insidious, and he'd let himself become attached to her on a deeper level than he'd ever intended.

He glanced at Cheri, dozing next to him in the fading afternoon sun. She was so warm and beautiful! He'd better start disentangling himself from her soon, before he got in so deep that there was no going back.

A feeling of chaos came over him, and he looked away from her, staring up at the blue sky. He hoped he had determination enough. He'd better get tough with himself if he was ever going to find his way back to his old, *real* life.

Cheri studied the small calendar in the kitchen, counting weeks and getting nervous. She hadn't been paying much attention to her periods, and she realized now that she hadn't had one in a couple of months. Skipping one hadn't concerned her much; it had happened before. But now she'd missed two in a row. Sometimes she felt a little queasy in the morning and her breasts had swollen a bit.

She considered telling Jake about it, but quickly decided not to. He'd changed in the last week or so, become slightly distant around her, even though they'd continued making love. She wondered if he was growing tired of her. Better not tell him anything until she was sure. She phoned the drugstore she used in Anacortes and ordered a home pregnancy test.

That evening, as they sat at the kitchen table having dinner, she asked, "Is Jasper still coming to visit next week?" Jasper had told them a month ago in a phone call that he'd be coming to San Francisco on business and would fly up briefly to see them again while he was on the West Coast.

"As far as I know. I'll call tonight and ask." Jake continued eating, not looking at her, and she felt once more that sense of coolness and distance from him, as if he'd made up his mind for some reason not to be close to her in any other way but physical.

It was strange. A few weeks ago, she'd begun to feel sure they were actually in love—not just the certain knowledge that she loved him, but the strong suspicion that he returned the emotion. They'd been so at one with each other, so happy during the past few months. The tensions and hang-ups that had once come between them had vanished. They'd shared worries and successes in their separate endeavors. She now knew more about meteorology than she'd ever dreamed she would and thought it fascinating. Jake reviewed her business math problems and had begun to help her envision what her café might be like, where to locate it and how to advertise.

It had been as if they were really married.

And then, suddenly, he began to behave as if he were rather disinterested. As the week had worn on, he talked less and less with her about his project and seemed reluctant to discuss her correspondence-course material with her. He hadn't been eating as much, either, she noticed, and wondered if perhaps he wasn't feeling well.

As she cut her meat, she carefully asked, "Do you suppose Jasper will still harbor any hope that we'll stay married? You pretty well discouraged him about that when he visited on your birthday."

"My dad never gives up hope," Jake said.

She wet her lips, trying to prepare herself for an answer she wouldn't like. "What will you tell him?"

He glanced at her sharply, as if wondering why she was asking that question. "I'll tell him we're sticking to our one-year agreement."

The reply stung. She lowered her eyes and nodded.

"We are, aren't we?" he asked, testing her.

Cheri didn't know how to answer. Should she tell him she wanted to stay married? "If that's what you want," she said.

He exhaled. "Don't be evasive. Isn't that what you want?"

She attempted to smile. "I've enjoyed being married to you. It seems . . . sad that it has to end. Does it have to?"

A myriad of subtle, changing expressions passed through his eyes and over his face. He looked confused, but he sounded positive as he replied, "That was our agreement, Cheri. It's been nice, but it's not what I planned for my future. Neither did you."

"Plans can change," she said.

"If you have your eyes on a goal, it's not good to step onto shifting sand because the sand looks attractive. You wind up shifting your life around and your goal gets lost in the shuffle. I can't let that happen to me." He studied her, as if trying to see if he'd gotten through to her. When she didn't say anything, he asked, "Why are you bringing this up? You aren't trying to undermine our original agreement, are you?"

"Not on purpose. But I have to admit my feelings have changed since we first started this arrangement. I like living with you and sleeping with you . . . sharing with you—"

"Yes, the sex is pleasant. But it's not essential," he interrupted. "There are much more important things to take into consideration when making your life plans."

"I thought it had developed into more than just a physical relationship," she ventured, her heart beating with apprehension, knowing she might be rejected.

His eyes narrowed and his chest began to rise and fall as his breathing grew irregular. "Now I suppose you're going to say you've fallen in love with me! How convenient. I once suspected you wanted to stay married to me so you'd have no more money worries.''

"No, Jake!" she objected, but he kept right on.

"What's that old saying? It's as easy to fall in love with a rich man as a poor man." He picked up his napkin and threw it on the table. "That's it, isn't it? That's what you've been up to all along. You lured me into a sexual relationship, and now you want to lure me into keeping this 'marriage' permanent."

Hot tears sprang into her eyes and began sliding down her cheeks. "How can you say that?"

"Ah, now we have tears, too. Sorry," he said, getting up from the table, "I refuse to be manipulated by female emotion!"

He stalked out the kitchen door, leaving her alone in the house. Cheri sat at the table, wiping her tears in silence, wondering how she could have ever thought a man so suspicious and insensitive might have fallen in love. She'd only been a sex toy to him all this time. He'd never come to value her at all. What was she going to do now, if she was pregnant?

A few days later, Pulse arrived with their weekly supplies. He seemed to notice that she looked sad, but with Jake silently hulking around, the pilot said little to her. After he flew off and Jake was out of the house, she found the home pregnancy kit she'd ordered in a white bag with the drugstore's logo. She went into the bathroom and used it. In minutes she knew.

She was, indeed, pregnant.

Now she sorely regretted all those times they had skipped using a condom. They'd gotten so used to spontaneity, to enjoying sex immediately, whenever the lusty urge came on them, that they hadn't always bothered to stop and find the package of prophylactics she'd ordered months ago at Jake's direction. They'd been irresponsible, and now she was paying for it in a life-altering way.

She ought to tell Jake. But he'd been so cold toward her ever since their argument at dinner that she didn't feel she could. He would only think she'd gotten pregnant on purpose, so he would feel he *had* to stay married to her. The last thing she wanted was for him to feel obligated to remain her husband. Clearly, he didn't love her as she loved him. Their situation was hopeless.

She realized with pain that she had to get away from him, so he wouldn't find out. She couldn't stand to hear his accusations, if he did learn the truth. This meant she had to leave the island, and soon—before her stomach began to get round.

Jake paced outside the house, looking at the sky, waiting to catch sight of Pulse's plane flying his father to see them. The marriage his dad had arranged had taken a miserable turn for the worse. Cheri and he were barely speaking. He'd hoped to disconnect from her gradually, with some dignity. Instead, he'd wound up making accusations about her motives he wasn't even convinced were true. Yet he felt reluctant to apologize, fearing he'd only be pulled back into their relationship that much more strongly. He'd decided it was best to keep his distance, now that their physical relationship had ended.

Jake knew he was in for it from his father, however. Cheri and he wouldn't be able to hide the deep rift between them. Jasper would no doubt try to play the Jimmy Carter role and offer to arbitrate their differences. Jake would rather finish out their remaining four months of contrived wedlock without his father's efforts to get them back on pleasant terms. Thank God Jasper didn't know that they'd actually fallen into a sexual relationship! If he found that out, he'd try even harder to keep them together. Jake hoped Cheri wouldn't say anything to let that information slip. Since she'd barely looked at him for the last few days, he didn't think it wise to broach the subject with her. He had no idea how she would behave. She'd been so erratic lately, sometimes in tears, sometimes remote and serene, spending lots of time in her room. Unfortunately, today the chips would just have to fall where they may.

In a few minutes, the plane came in sight, and Jake went down to the pier to meet it. He helped Jasper out of the aircraft. Pulse flew off again, and Jake took his father to the house.

Jasper was his usual congenial self, and he looked well. "Never got a haircut, did you?" he said to his son as they walked through the front door.

Jake lowered his gaze. Cheri had liked his hair long, so he'd never asked her to cut it. "I'll have Pulse fly me to Anacortes one of these days," he told Jasper.

At that moment, Cheri came from the kitchen and hurried to Jasper. She hugged him warmly and began to cry. Jake looked away.

"I'm so happy to see you," she said to Jasper, wiping her eyes. "We'll eat in about an hour. Why don't you and Jake have a look at the garden? I'll bring you some iced tea."

Jake followed her suggestion. As he and his father sat on a bench under a shady tree with their iced drinks, he decided honesty was the best policy with his father. "I'm afraid things have gone downhill between Cheri and me. It's too bad, but I told you it wouldn't work. If she seems . . . upset, that's probably why."

Jasper's black-brown eyes fixed on Jake. "Downhill? How far?"

"Rock bottom. We basically aren't speaking."

"That *is* down," Jasper said, shaking his head. "But you two seemed so compatible."

"Not really. She's young, with a different lifestyle than I have. I'm academic. She's...she's all over the place. Confused, I think," Jake said, knowing that that word probably applied to him more than her. But he needed to bluff his father a bit. "Living together has gotten pretty difficult."

"You're sure it's not living with *you* that's gotten difficult?" Jasper said.

"Maybe." Jake tried to sound as if he had some equanimity on the subject. "It may be because I'm just not cut out for marriage. At least not yet—not for a long time."

Jasper processed this statement, his eyes sharp and inquisitive, making Jake wonder what conclusions he was drawing. His father never seemed to be able to take a statement at face value.

Jake ignored him and changed the subject, giving his dad an earful about the progress of his meteorological study, so as to avoid any further conversation about the doomed marriage Jasper had arranged.

Jasper was yawning by the time Cheri called them in for dinner. After they were seated and Cheri had served the elaborate meal she'd made, they ate in silence for a while. Jake noted Jasper eyeing them both, as if measuring their demeanors and silently scoping them out. All at once his father complimented Cheri on her cooking.

"Delicious roast lamb," he said. "It's so flavorful and tender. How did you prepare it?"

Cheri seemed distracted, as if she couldn't remember. "I...marinated it in wine and spices. Then I cooked it slowly for hours. That's why it's tender."

"Too bad you can't use that method on Jake once in a while, eh?" Jasper said, joking.

For the first time Cheri smiled, almost laughed. "Yes, it's too bad, but it probably wouldn't have worked. He's got a tough hide."

Jake silently cut his meat, unsure where this conversation was going. He hadn't heard Cheri say this much in days.

"Jasper," she said, putting down her fork with some gravity, "I . . . have a favor to ask."

Jake glanced up, hearing a strange hush in her voice.

"I'd like you to take me back to Chicago with you," she told Jasper.

Jake nearly dropped his knife. He stopped breathing.

Jasper's countenance changed, taking on a grave expression. "But why, my dear?"

"I just can't stay here anymore. You probably can tell by observing us that Jake and I are—are simply not getting along. I don't feel I can go through with this marriage bargain. I know our year isn't up, so I'm willing to forfeit the money you'd offered to pay me for marrying Jake. I—I just basically want out. That's all." She shrugged in a poignant way. "That's it."

Jake began to feel slightly dizzy and realized he hadn't been breathing. He took a long breath and leaned back limply in his chair. He'd never expected Cheri to just walk out. And forfeit her money, too. Was this some kind of new strategy?

"You realize," Jasper said gently, "that if you leave the marriage now, Jake's university department won't get the money I promised, either."

Cheri's aqua eyes grew troubled. "It's me who's walking out. Why punish him?"

Jake felt embarrassed at hearing her argue on his behalf. She sounded so genuine that it didn't seem like any strategy. She was even taking the blame. And he had accused her of being mercenary, of wanting to stay married to him for his money. He felt like a heel. She was a better person than he.

"It's my fault," Jake interjected. "I'm the one who doesn't want to be married. I've made life unpleasant for her. Why don't you just keep your money, Dad, and we'll all go our separate ways? It's the best solution—that way nobody owes anybody anything. We'll just chalk it up to experience."

Jake glanced at Cheri and noticed tears sliding down her face as she stared at the table. She looked so terribly sad. He wondered why. Had she really grown that fond of living with him? Jake had the uneasy inkling that once she was gone, he was going to experience a loss he couldn't even begin to fathom. Why was she in such a hurry?

Jasper gave her his handkerchief. "Don't cry, Cheri. Don't be upset. It's not good for you. We'll all get through this," he soothed. "You have to keep up your strength."

She took the handkerchief and wiped the tears from her face, but said brokenly, "We won't get through this. It's all over."

"It only seems that way," Jasper said.

"No, it *is*," she insisted, new tears flowing. "You don't understand, Jasper. I have to leave this island. Now."

Jasper put his finger on his mouth and seemed momentarily annoyed with himself. "I'm sorry. I wasn't trying to talk you into staying. Of course you may leave with me tonight. I simply meant that…you will be happy again someday. I'll see to it."

She searched Jasper's eyes, as if questioning him. Jasper smiled, and her face took on a mystified expression.

What the hell is going on between them? Jake wondered. *Why am I always the one left out?* Some nagging, angry voice deep inside told him that *he* ought to be the one comforting her with a look, not his dad.

Somehow they got through dinner. Cheri told Jasper her bags were all packed. She wondered if he could make arrangements for a ticket for her from Seattle to Chicago. Jasper assured her he would get her on the same plane he was flying back on, or he'd book them both a new flight.

"Can I bring my cat, too?"

"Of course!" Jasper replied. "We'll book her a seat, too."

As Cheri smiled with relief, Jake felt increasingly lost and confused.

"So... what do you want me to do?" he asked his father. "Stay here? Go back to Madison?"

"That's up to you," Jasper said coolly. "What do you want to do?"

"Finish my study here on the island," Jake replied. He did want to finish the study. More than that, he felt he needed time alone to get himself together before returning to university life.

"Then stay out the year here," Jasper said. "I've already provided most of the money for the grant I arranged for you. I'll continue providing for you to finish. I talked you into coming here, so I owe you that. Is that satisfactory?"

"Fine."

"Good." Jasper glanced at his watch. "The seaplane will be coming back in a half hour, Cheri. We'd better start taking your things out to the pier." He glanced disparagingly at his son. "Leave the dirty dishes for Jake to clean up."

Later, when the plane had arrived and they were all on the pier loading her luggage and the cat carrier, Cheri turned to Jake and held out her hand.

"Goodbye. Sorry it ended this way." Her face had a taut look, as if she were working hard to contain her emotions.

He took her hand. "I am, too. I wish you could have discussed this with me, instead of leaving so abruptly."

"You were angry," she said. "We weren't speaking. How could I?"

He didn't have a good answer. "Will you call me from Chicago? I don't feel right just leaving things like this."

She stared at him for a long moment, the look in her eyes doubtful. "Maybe," she replied.

He knew she wouldn't. "I'd like to know where you are, where you go," he said, following her as she walked toward the plane to board it. Jasper had already gotten into the craft.

"I'll contact you," she assured him. She swallowed hard. "Bye." With that, she got into the plane, and Pulse shut the door. In moments the craft was skimming the water, then gliding into the air. Soon it was only a speck on the horizon. Then it disappeared.

Jake walked back into the empty house, feeling bleak with shock and totally bereft. It seemed to him as if his life had ended.

The next evening, Jake was sitting at the kitchen table, picking at his meal of leftover lamb, when the phone rang. He sprang from the table to get it, hoping it might be Cheri. Instead, he heard his father's voice.

"Oh. Hi, Dad."

"You don't sound very chipper," Jasper said with amusement.

Jake swallowed the jibe and asked, "How's Cheri? Where is she?"

"At a hotel. Bea and I offered to let her stay here, but she wouldn't. I found an apartment for her today. She'll move in soon. She called a little while ago and said she'd gotten back her old job at Tucci's. I offered to find her a job in an office, but she doesn't like taking help from me."

"What hotel is she at?" Jake asked.

"She made me swear not to tell you."

"Can't you tell me anyway?"

"No, I won't break my word to her. You had your chance with her and you blew it, Jake. Must be pretty lonely there on that island."

Jake grew provoked by his father's needling. It made him stubborn. "I'll get over it!"

"Too bad, if you do."

"What the hell does that mean?"

"Finding a woman who loves you for yourself isn't so easy. You had that and threw it away."

Jake remembered Cheri's hint that she cared for him. "How do you know? Did she say she loved me?"

"No. But on the plane home she kept worrying how you would eat, how you would take care of yourself, now that she was gone."

"Then why did she leave?" Jake asked.

"For a brilliant scientist, and a man who's had an innate understanding of mathematics since he was a boy, you sure have a hard time putting two and two together," Jasper said.

Jake clenched his jaw. "Okay, I'll bite. What equation am I missing here?"

"She left because she didn't think *you* loved *her*," Jasper said, slowly enunciating each word, as if Jake was a little dim.

"Maybe...she was right," Jake said.

"Was she?"

Somehow the words *yes, she was right* just couldn't form in his mouth. "Even if I do love her, it doesn't mean we should stay married. I never wanted to get married in the first place—to anyone! I have my own vision of what I think my future should be. If you hadn't interfered, I would still be on track."

"You have a vision, all right," Jasper agreed. "Tunnel vision. All you see are your goals. Everything else, including a beautiful, sincere woman who loves you, you view as extraneous." He sighed. "Well, if that's how you want to live, then I certainly won't interfere ever again. I do have to admire your resolve. You take after me that way. I'm sure you'll have a brilliant career, Jake. But at the end of your life, what else will you have?''

''I'll get married and have kids when I'm fifty,'' Jake argued, disliking the way his father was writing off his whole life.

''Cheri will be long married to some other man by then.''

The prediction gave Jake a harrowing chill, as if someone had thrown a bucket of cold water on him. He knew Jasper was right. Men would sell their souls to marry her.

''You expect that there will be another woman just waiting in the wings for you twenty years from now?'' Jasper railed. ''Being a millionaire's son, I suppose you'll never lack for potential wives. But will they marry a workaholic, middle-aged professor for love or for his money?''

''You're going to disinherit me, so I won't *be* rich,'' Jake reminded him, finding his wit again. ''I didn't stay married long enough to fulfill the terms of your will.''

There was silence on the phone. Jasper had apparently forgotten. ''Good point,'' he said grudgingly. ''All right. Then I'll call my lawyer and have him take that clause out. Bea never approved of it, anyway. No, Son, you *will* inherit your entire share. Even if you give it all away, you'll still be perceived as a millionaire by everyone. And when you *are* fifty, I hope you remember fondly the young woman—the wife—you let slip away, who wanted you for yourself. You might be interested to know that I tried and tried to convince her, but she refuses to take any money from me—not even the fifteen thousand she once suggested as a compromise figure. I paid the lease money on her apartment, and she's insisting she'll repay me every cent. It'll take her awhile, working at Tucci's, but she has integrity. One doesn't find that much anymore. Two decades from now, you may not find it at all.''

Jake held the phone at his ear, feeling numbed by his father's barrage.

"Are you there?" Jasper asked when he didn't respond.

"I'm here. You've given me a headache."

"Good," Jasper said. "I hope it's an indication you've started thinking!"

Jasper hung up the phone feeling frustrated. Cheri's stubborn insistence on going it alone worried him, and it seemed as though Jake might never come out of his scientific cocoon. And there was another major issue at hand that Jasper wasn't quite sure how to deal with. He'd need to enlist Bea's help. But he knew his wife was going to be upset with him.

He walked into the kitchen where she was mixing ingredients to put in the bread machine.

"Talked to Jake," Jasper said.

"How is he?"

"Lonely, I think." He sat on a stool by the counter and put on a smile. "I told him I'm taking that marriage clause out of my will. So he, and all our children, will inherit their shares whether they marry or not."

Bea paused, flour on her hands, and looked at him. "So you've finally seen the light, now that you've disrupted Jake's and Cheri's lives—now that they're both miserable! I hope you've learned from this not to interfere anymore."

"Yes, and you're absolutely right, Bea. As always."

She eyed him suspiciously. "Don't be so agreeable. It makes me wonder what you're up to. What *are* you up to?"

"Me? Nothing. Nothing at all. I've . . . learned my lesson. It's just that, now that Cheri, unfortunately, has left Jake, I believe that there may be a remaining issue. It may be good news, actually. But it will be an issue that you and I may have to help her deal with."

Bea leaned against the counter, forgetting her yeast dough. "Go on."

Jasper chewed his lip, considering how to reveal what he knew, but wasn't supposed to know. "I have a suspicion that Cheri is pregnant."

Bea's eyes widened and she straightened up. "When you brought her here from the airport, I thought she looked thinner than she used to, poor thing. Certainly not pregnant."

"I think it's early on. Maybe two, two and a half months."

"She's seen a doctor?"

"I doubt it."

"How do you know she's in a family way? Did she tell you?"

Jasper pursed his mouth. This was the sticky part Bea would certainly not like to hear. "No. You see, in my arrangement for Jake's scientific study on the island, I agreed to pay all the expenses for their stay there, including grocery store bills . . . and drugstore bills."

"Yes . . . ?" Bea said, sounding like she knew what was coming.

"So I asked the stores to send me the listings of the— the merchandise they purchased."

"Jasper, really! That's like spying on them."

"Yes, dear. Be that as it may, I . . . happened to notice that a few months ago, condoms were on the drugstore list. So I naturally assumed, and happily, too, that they'd begun—"

"I get the picture," Bea said. "And?"

"And then, just about a week ago, there was a listing for a home pregnancy test. And soon after that, coincidentally just when I visited them, Cheri suddenly wanted to leave. I'm suspecting that she's pregnant, doesn't want to tell Jake because she doesn't think he loves her and is trying to handle the situation on her own. So, what I was hoping, Bea, is that maybe you might talk to her and verify what I suspect. You know, woman-to-woman. I wouldn't feel right—"

"Wouldn't feel right? You manipulate them into a marriage, *hoping* for grandchildren, and now that the poor girl may be pregnant, you want me to help clean up the mess!"

Jasper hung his head. "Mea culpa, Bea. Guilty as charged. I should have listened to you." He looked up. "But there it is—that's the situation. And if she is going to have a baby, it's your grandchild as well as mine."

"And it's Jake's child. What about him?"

"He'll learn the news eventually. I'm still hoping he'll get his priorities straightened out before fatherhood straightens them out for him. It would be better that way."

Bea tapped her wooden spoon on the counter. "Jasper, Jasper, what am I going to do with you? You put our sons through such trials!"

"I prefer the word *challenges*, Bea. I challenge them to look at their lives differently."

"By maneuvering some unsuspecting young woman into their path."

"And letting nature take its course," Jasper said. "And I suspect nature *has* taken its course in Jake and

Cheri's case. I'm still hoping nature will draw them back together.''

"So do I," Bea said, shaking her head with concern. "So do I."

10

———◆———

Cheri sat with Jasper and Bea in the beautiful living room of their mansion after dinner. She'd never been in a home like this, and she felt a bit intimidated. Jasper had insisted she come for dinner tonight, saying he wanted to repay her for the dinners she'd cooked for him on the island. She would have rather been getting settled in her new apartment. It was her only night off from Tucci's.

Jasper got up, said he had a phone call to make and winked at his wife as he left the room. When he'd gone, Bea sighed and got up to sit next to Cheri on the couch.

"This is most embarrassing, Cheri, but I'd like to talk to you about something."

"Sure," Cheri said, on edge. She adored Jake's mother, but something in Bea's demeanor made her uneasy.

"Jasper...has a hunch that...well, that you're in a family way."

"Family way?" Cheri asked warily.

Bea chuckled. "It's an old-fashioned term. It means pregnant."

Cheri stared down at her hands in her lap, not knowing what to say. She hadn't told anyone yet, not knowing for sure what to do. But she supposed she'd have to tell the Derrings sometime. Eventually, she'd have to tell Jake, too.

Tears filled her eyes. "It's true," she whispered. "I am. I'm sorry."

Bea smiled and stroked her arm. "Don't be sorry, Cheri. You've done nothing wrong. You are legally married to our son. I'm certainly happy to have another grandchild come into the world. Jasper's been secretly beaming about it for days."

"How did he figure it out?" Cheri asked. "I'm still thin."

Bea hesitated. "Jasper seems to have a sixth sense sometimes. Some of us wish he'd keep it to himself, but he never does."

Cheri smiled and wiped her eyes. "Well, actually, now that you know, I'm relieved."

"Have you seen a doctor?"

"Yes. He said I looked fine and gave me some vitamin supplements to take. I've been taking them every day. Fortunately, I don't have too much trouble with morning sickness. It hasn't interfered with my work schedule."

All at once, Jasper reappeared in the room. His face was bright. "Something going on?" he asked. "You're both smiling."

"Oh, Jasper, don't pretend you weren't in the next room listening," Bea chided him.

Jasper looked only slightly embarrassed. "All right, I was. So we can expect another grandchild?"

Cheri nodded. "I just wish I could have stayed married to Jake."

"You still are married," Jasper said. "I haven't given up hope that—"

"I filed for divorce," Cheri told him. "Jake should be getting the papers in a few days. It's not final yet. But the marriage will be ended soon."

"Oh." Jasper looked deflated and sat down.

"He'd think I got pregnant on purpose, to make him feel that he *had* to stay married to me," she explained. "I don't want him to think that. It may even be true—I don't know. Maybe unconsciously that's why I wasn't careful. Maybe I wanted to have his baby. But I don't want him to think I was trying to manipulate him. I didn't mean to."

"I'm sure you didn't," Bea said. "You really do love Jake, don't you?"

"Yes," Cheri replied. "But he never felt that way about me. It was just...you know, a physical thing on his part. He always made it very clear that he didn't want a permanent relationship. I was silly enough to hope he would change. But he has his own plans." She paused and gathered her emotions. In a brighter tone, she said, "I'll raise the baby myself. You both can see him or her anytime. I'll be working, so I may need baby-sitters," she said with a chuckle. "And Jake can see the baby, too, when he wants. If he wants."

"Whatever happens," Jasper said, "for the time being, you must allow us to pay your medical expenses. We want the best care for our grandchild. I'll set up a trust fund for the child's education, too."

Cheri rubbed her forehead. She didn't like taking money, but she knew having a baby would be expensive. She wanted the best for her child, just as they did. "All right," she agreed reluctantly. "But only for the baby. I don't want anything for myself. Jake would think—"

"Never mind what Jake would think," Jasper said. "He's forgotten how to think straight, anyway."

Jake was walking down the ridge, having just sent up a weather balloon, when he saw Pulse's seaplane flying low over the water toward the pier. He walked down to meet the pilot.

"How you doing, Jake?" Pulse said as he got out of the plane.

"Fine." Jake helped tie the craft to the pier.

"Must be lonely out here without Cheri. Sure surprised me when she left."

"Me, too."

"She coming back?"

"Probably not," Jake said curtly. "Why don't you just leave the supplies here on the pier? I'll take them into the house myself."

"Whatever you say," Pulse agreed. After the boxes and bags of goods were moved from the seaplane to the dock, the pilot handed him a bundle of mail tied with string. "Here's what the post office had for you."

As Pulse flew off, Jake stood on the pier looking through the mail, hoping to find a letter from Cheri. He hadn't heard a word from her. If it weren't for news from his father, he wouldn't even know where she was or if she was alive. He hoped she might at least write him a letter.

He found none. But he did find an envelope from a law firm in Chicago. Curious, he opened it. His temper ignited as he read it. How dare she just go off and file for divorce! Without even so much as a warning.

But then he remembered that he'd always insisted he didn't want to stay married. No doubt she thought there was no reason to discuss it. Maybe she'd decided she'd show him just who was the more anxious to get divorced. In any case, the letter made it quite clear she no longer had any regard for him or his feelings.

Well, why should she? Jake asked himself as he lugged boxes from the pier into the house. He'd disregarded *her* feelings. He wished now he'd been more sensitive toward her, instead of putting up defenses to keep her at arm's length emotionally.

He felt banished here on this island—so *alone*. And the banishment was of his own making. He hadn't wanted her to stay in his life, but now that he'd chased her away with his callous behavior, he wished he'd been wise enough to recognize and cherish what he'd had. He wished she'd come back. But he didn't even have an address or phone number to reach her and tell her. His father stubbornly guarded her secrecy, which Jake thought was odd. He'd thought Jasper wanted to see them get back together. Maybe his dad was giving up on him, too.

Jake slumped at the kitchen table after putting the groceries away. He couldn't go on like this. He didn't even care about his study of the microclimate anymore. Nothing seemed to mean anything or be worthwhile pursuing. His life felt empty, like a vacuum that only Cheri could fill. He'd told himself it was all physical, that he could let go. But now that she'd let *him* go, the pain made him realize that his emotions *were* involved. Deeply involved. He'd broken up with other women and had always recovered quickly. This was different.

This was love. He'd never been in love before. No wonder he hadn't recognized the feeling sooner.

He had to tell her. There must be some way to find her. A light bulb went on in his head. He sat up straight, remembering that his dad had said she'd gone back to work at Tucci's.

He went to the phone, called Directory Service and got the phone number for the pizzeria. Knowing it was late afternoon in Chicago, he dialed the restaurant, hoping she'd be there.

"Tucci's," a male voice answered.

"Is Cheri in?" Jake asked.

"Who's calling?"

Jake hesitated. "Her husband."

"She's married?"

"Tell her Jake wants to talk to her," he snapped in an authoritative manner.

"Oh," the man said, as if recognizing the name. "She's made it clear to everyone that if *Jake* called, she didn't want to talk to him."

Jake's jaw dropped. My God! Why was she taking such measures to avoid him? "Let me speak to the manager."

"*I'm* Sam, the manager. I don't like my waitresses to take personal phone calls on the job, anyway. So I believe *this* phone call is finished."

"Wait—" A click on the line effectively shut Jake up. "Damn!" he exclaimed. Dude was sitting on the floor watching him. The cat's sleepy eyes widened at his master's angry tone. "She's not getting away with this," Jake said to the cat as he paced the kitchen. "She can't just run out on me, now that I'm in love with her, and hit me with divorce papers without any preparation or explanation. She didn't even give me time to change my mind about staying married! *Women* are always allowed to change their mind. Can't a man? She could have hung around a little longer and given me the chance! What the hell is the matter with her?" He shouted the last question so sharply that Dude ran out of the room.

Two days later Cheri was sitting behind the cash register at Tucci's, a station to which Sam had relegated her. Once he'd found out that she'd been married, and began to notice the maternity tops Bea had insisted on giving her as a gift, he began to treat her nervously. It was as if he were constantly afraid that she'd have the baby on the spot, even though her stomach was only just starting to protrude. He insisted she take the cash register, so she could sit down often.

Sam's concern surprised Cheri. He'd always tended to be gruff. On the other hand, perhaps now that he knew she had a connection with the Derring family, he figured he'd better treat her with deference.

She didn't like special treatment, but she didn't argue. Her doctor had told her it wasn't good for her to be on her feet constantly. It was 4:00 p.m. and she'd just opened up the cash register for the usual evening crowd, though the restaurant was practically empty at the moment. She was in the process of counting dollar bills when someone came up to the register. In the midst of her tally, she didn't look up right away.

"How was your dinner?" she asked automatically, without losing her count.

"I haven't had a decent meal in weeks."

The familiar voice came as a jolt. "Jake!" Her eyes locked with his. Her heart rate shot into high gear.

"Hello to you, too!" he said. His dark brown eyes were staring at her rather accusingly. She sensed he was so full of tension, he was almost shaking.

"What are you doing in Chicago?"

"I came to see you! You haven't even tried to contact me. My parents and you have some conspiracy going so that I can't even get a phone number or address to reach you. So here I am."

"Why?"

"*Why?* Because you—you just flew off and left, like an uncaged bird. No explanation. Barely a goodbye. Then I get divorce papers!"

"Isn't that what you wanted?" she asked.

"Not necessarily. You could have asked what I wanted instead of assuming."

"But you always said you didn't want to stay married."

"Well, you could have asked me again before running off, just to make sure!"

Sam came up. "Something wrong here?" he asked, looking at Jake sharply.

Cheri put the dollar bills she'd never finished counting back into the register. "This is my ex-husband—"

"Not yet!" Jake interrupted.

"This is Jake Derring," she said.

Sam's manner instantly changed at the mention of the name Derring. "Oh. Then why don't you two sit down at a table? I'll get someone else to take care of the cash register."

Cheri grew annoyed at Sam's deferential manner, but didn't protest. She got up from the register and walked around the counter.

Jake eyed her long blouse, which had blue-and-pink alphabet letters embroidered across the front. "Have you taken on another new style? From bulky sweatshirts to sexy T-shirts to ladylike smocks. Is this a new sort of clothing rebellion?"

Cheri ignored the comment for the time being and led him to a table in a corner of the restaurant. After they'd sat down, she asked, "Why do you want to see me? Why are you here?"

He raked his hand through his thick black hair, still long and appealingly rumpled. "It's not the same without you. I wanted to talk to you about—about reconsidering this divorce thing."

Cheri was afraid to hope. She asked him with doubt in her tone, "You're saying you'd actually like to *stay* married?"

"Yes. I think we should give it another try."

"But why, Jake?" she asked, shaking her head in a despairing manner. "You don't love me."

"Are you crazy? Of course I love you!" he retorted. "You don't love *me,* or you wouldn't have run off."

"That's ridiculous!" she protested. "I've always loved you! But I didn't think that was something you ever wanted to hear."

They stared at one another, processing what the other was saying, realizing they were arguing when actually they were in beautiful agreement.

Jake smiled and looked into her eyes, his gaze rueful. "I was a fool. I didn't appreciate what I had when you were with me. I didn't know I was falling in love."

She studied him for a long moment, hesitating. This still seemed too good to be true. She must be misunderstanding him somehow. This moment couldn't last. "You *do* love me?"

"Yes! I'm begging you to come back to me. I'll—I'll get down on my knees...." He began to get up from the table.

"Jake—"

All at once he was on his knees beside her, looking up at her. "Will you come back?" he cajoled, taking her hand warmly in his. "What can I do? How can I convince you? I love you! Fly back to the island with me. We'll finish the year, and then I want you to come with me to Wisconsin. You'll be near the campus. You can take university classes and not have to do correspondence courses. You won't have to be a waitress. You can do whatever you want. Just so you live with me again and make love with me. I'm dying without you," he said in a desperate voice.

Tears gathered in her eyes. "Thank you for saying that, Jake, but—"

"Don't you believe me?"

She paused a moment. "Yes," she said with a bit of surprise, "I do. But, Jake, will you sit down again? There's something you need to know, and it's going to be kind of a shock."

Jake's relieved expression grew anxious again. As he got up, he said, "You've met someone else?" He searched her face for answers as he sat down opposite her again. "You're secretly in love with Pulse? You're my parents' long-lost daughter? What?"

She laughed at his suggestions. "No, I'm not in love with Pulse, and I wish I'd had parents like yours. But you could say I've met someone new."

His complexion paled. "Who is he?"

"It might be a she. I'm going to have a baby. Yours."

He stared at her, dumbfounded, the color coming back into his face. "You're pregnant?" He broke into a huge smile. "That's wonderful!" He leaned toward her. "That's great! Why would you want to divorce me now?"

"I never did want a divorce. But I was afraid you'd think I got pregnant to keep us married. I wanted to divorce you quickly, so you'd never be able to think that of me."

Jake's forehead constricted in vertical lines, as if he were feeling acute inner pain. "I've been so stupid. I accused you of trying to manipulate me. I tried to shut you out. That's why you didn't feel you could approach me, isn't it?"

She nodded. Tears filled her eyes again and she looked down, feeling an ache inside, too. "Maybe I *was* trying to hold on to you. I wanted your baby. I didn't try very hard not to get pregnant."

He reached across the table and brushed away a tear from her cheek. "I wasn't very diligent about contraception, either. Maybe unconsciously I wanted you to be pregnant so you'd be bonded to me permanently. Maybe that's why we made love constantly—one reason, anyway," he said with a twinkle in his eyes. "My heart already knew what my head kept resisting. I loved you to distraction. Still do. And I love the distraction. Can't live without it now."

She smiled. "What about your goal to save the planet?"

"The planet can go to pieces. You're all I care about."

Cheri took hold of his hand. "You can have both, you know. You'll have me, our child and two cats, and I'd bet a bundle you'll find a way to save the earth, too. You're a brilliant man. You can do anything!"

"Maybe you're right," he said, bringing her hand to his mouth. He kissed her palm soundly. "Now that I've gotten rid of my tunnel vision, I've got it all. Remember the birthday wish you asked me to make? At the time, I thought wishes were stupid, but I said to myself, 'Let me get through this year without losing myself.' Well, I found myself and a lot more—all because of you. I found love and joy and the richness of life. *You* are my life." His voice broke with emotion and he glanced around the restaurant. "Can we get out of here?"

Cheri blinked back tears and grinned. "Okay. I guess if I'm going back to the island with you, I'll have to quit my job again, anyway."

"Quit!" Jake said. "You have an apartment nearby?"

"Yes."

"Let's go, make love, get you packed and catch the first plane to Seattle."

"Sounds perfect. Oh, Jake," she said, squeezing his hand, "I love you so much. I'm so happy you came here to find me."

"I am, too. We had a close call. But I love you too much to lose you without a fight. I won't ever lose you again." He rose from the table, pulling on her hand. "Come on—our island is waiting!"

Jasper squinted out the front window of his Mercedes-Benz. "For heaven's sake!" he said aloud.

"What?" Bea asked, sitting beside him, unbuckling her seat belt. They'd just parked in Tucci's lot.

"Look!" Jasper said, pointing.

Bea leaned forward. "It looks like Cheri . . . and Jake! I almost wouldn't know him. His hair is so long."

"It worked," Jasper marveled. "It actually worked!"

"What worked?"

"My plan. He came back for her. They're rushing off, holding hands. They're probably going to her place."

Bea smiled. "I hope so. I guess we'd better not disturb them just now. Maybe they'll stop to see us later."

"I did it, I did it, I did it," Jasper sang to himself merrily. "Gosh, I'm getting good at this!"

Bea set her elbow on the narrow ledge of the door window, propping her head against her fingertips. "Jasper, he came back on his own, and they've obviously worked it out on their own. How can you pretend to take credit?"

"But it's the positive energy I put into needlepointing their wedding pillow, Bea. Once you set an idea in motion, the universe takes care of it. I seem to have really gotten the hang of it! Two kids married off in a row. One grandchild and another on the way. God, I'm good at this!"

Bea stared at him, drawing in a deep breath. "Jasper, before you start planning which of our children will be your next victim, let's have some pizza. I need to keep up my strength if I'm going to keep up with you."

"I know, Bea. I'm just a matchmaking marvel, aren't I?"

"Matchmaking menace, I'd say. Pizza, Jasper. Let's go."

* * * * *

FORTUNE'S Children™

Bestselling Author

LISA JACKSON

Continues the twelve-book series—FORTUNE'S CHILDREN
in August 1996 with Book Two

THE MILLIONAIRE AND THE COWGIRL

When playboy millionaire Kyle Fortune inherited a Wyoming
ranch from his grandmother, he never expected to come
face-to-face with Samantha Rawlings, the willful woman
he'd never forgotten…and the daughter he'd never known.
Although Kyle enjoyed his jet-setting life-style, Samantha and
Caitlyn made him yearn for hearth and home.

MEET THE FORTUNES—a family whose legacy is greater than
riches. Because where there's a will…there's a *wedding!*

*A CASTING CALL TO
ALL FORTUNE'S CHILDREN FANS!*
If you are truly one of the fortunate
few, you may win a trip to
Los Angeles to audition for
Wheel of Fortune®. Look for
details in all retail Fortune's Children titles!

FC-2-C-R

Who can resist a Texan...or a Calloway?

This September, award-winning author
ANNETTE BROADRICK
returns to Texas, with a brand-new
story about the Calloways...

SONS OF TEXAS

Rogues and Ranchers

CLINT: The brave leader. Used to keeping secrets.

CADE: The Lone Star Stud. Used to having women fall at his feet...

MATT: The family guardian. Used to handling trouble...

They must discover the identity of the mystery woman with Calloway eyes—and uncover a conspiracy that threatens their family....

Look for **SONS OF TEXAS**: Rogues and Ranchers in September 1996!

Only from Silhouette...where passion lives.

You can run, but you cannot
hide...from love.

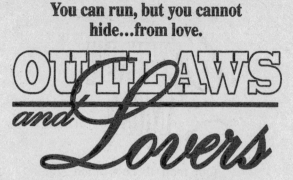

OUTLAWS
and Lovers

This August, experience danger, excitement and
love on the run with three couples thrown
together by life-threatening circumstances.

Enjoy three complete stories by some of your
favorite authors—all in one special collection!

THE PRINCESS AND THE PEA
by Kathleen Korbel

IN SAFEKEEPING
by Naomi Horton

FUGITIVE
by Emilie Richards

Available this August wherever books are sold.

Silhouette®

Look us up on-line at:http://www.romance.net

The dynasty begins.

LINDA HOWARD
The Mackenzies

Now available for the first time, Mackenzie's Mountain and Mackenzie's Mission, together in one affordable, trade-size edition. Don't miss out on the two stories that started it all!

Mackenzie's Mountain: Wolf Mackenzie is a loner. All he cares about is his ranch and his son. Labeled a half-breed by the townspeople, he chooses to stay up on his mountain—that is, until the spunky new schoolteacher decides to pay the Mackenzies a visit. And that's when all hell breaks loose.

Mackenzie's Misson: Joe "Breed" Mackenzie is a colonel in the U.S. Air Force. All he cares about is flying. He is the best of the best and determined never to let down his country—even for love. But that was before he met a beautiful civilian engineer, who turns his life upside down.

Available this August, at your favorite retail outlet.